It's not always Murder
Karl Wilder

It's not Always Murder

A John Evans mystery, Volume 1

Karl Wilder

Published by Vintage Pulp Press, 2024.

IT'S NOT ALWAYS MURDER

First edition. July 16, 2024.

ISBN: 979-8224939503

Written by Karl Wilder.

Also by Karl Wilder

A John Evans mystery
It's not Always Murder
You Can Get A Man With A Gun

For Marion May who told me I could and my brother
Tom who has supported me in all my incarnations

It's Not Always Murder

August 11, 2000. Wanted: Men or Women with no current reason for existence in this life for a very rare assignment. Because of the nature of our work, we cannot go into full detail in this advertisement. If you feel you have nothing to lose and want an exciting future, please respond, and you will be contacted for a meeting.

I read the above notice with cynicism and quickly dismissed it as a scam. Even the e-mail address was Gmail, which is consistent with scammers.

However, it hit me in the face like a bucket of ice water.

33-year-old white male... Average height, lower than average weight in the current obese society, and due to my Turkish ancestors, I was covered in fur, somewhat like a gorilla; all my hair and a pleasant enough face, good straight teeth, and I fucking hated my life.

I was an only child, and both parents were dead. I had never met the extended family and would have to get a DNA test to determine if they even existed.

I had a job and okay pay: the Food Purchasing agent at a hotel. I spent my days confirming counts, receiving orders, placing orders and being bored out of my fucking skull. My parents left me enough money to buy a small apartment. I never went hungry. My only respite was the daily workouts that moved me out of my head into my body.

Women came and went, but none stayed long enough to develop a real relationship. Women love to talk, and I am not one for listening. I tune out prattle.

Objectively, I had nothing to be miserable about, and I was not unhappy, but I was not happy.

I wanted excitement and travel, and my two-week-a-year vacation did not give me enough time to really know the world.

Name: Jonathan Olaysiz.

Maybe I was responding to scammers, but I sent an email; I truly felt I had nothing to lose.

Chapter 2

Three weeks later, my phone rang just as I had finished getting dressed.

"Mr. Olaysiz, this is Jeff Kimball from the B.P.R.D. We received your email. We had many responses, so it took time to go through them all." He had a slight English accent, which was not what I expected.

My guard was up. "If you had so many people, why would you contact me? What stood out about my email?"

"Absolutely nothing, which is why we are contacting you. Your message was as blank as I suspect you feel your life is, and we would like to talk with you. My colleague Mrs Miles and I, if you have time for a coffee or a drink?"

They wanted to meet in public, not too scary. "How about tonight, Glueck Brewing, downtown Minneapolis at 6:30." I lived in St. Paul, but they were not coming near my neighbourhood until I knew what this was about.

"That's only about a 3-hour flight; we can make that."

"Where are you coming from?"

"Washington, D.C., you might want to look us up. We are an official government agency. "

I looked them up, and it was a fictional agency created by the Marvel Comic world. This meeting was going to be fun.

I went to work as usual, got through my day, and then drove to Minneapolis. When I walked into the bar, I knew immediately who they were. At the end of the day, the ties loosened, the jackets came off, and these two were so buttoned up I thought they might explode.

"Mr Kimball and Mrs. Miles, I presume?" He was a thin white man in a perfectly tailored suit. She, a voluptuous blonde of about 50, was in a pantsuit designed to hide all of her natural features but failing miserably.

I took a seat, and we ordered. Two coffees and one whisky, they were working after all.

"I looked up your agency; it is fictional, so who are you?"

Miles fielded this: "We don't exist, officially, and the only way to give you an idea of what we do is to use the fictional name. We work for the government and investigate and instigate the paranormal." She showed me what looked like a government ID with name, address, photo, magnetic chip, and no department listed.

"You are not inspiring confidence."

Kimball chipped in, and the accent gave him credibility the words lacked. "We believe we can offer you an entirely new life, not a new job, a new life in a place and time you have never experienced."

"Go on."

"We were conducting an experiment in detachment, letting go of the obvious Matrix of life with a series of meditations. We were working with a local volunteer in Washington. As we were working with her, she disappeared. When we went to her home, someone else responded to our knock, claiming she had woken in this bed, in this house, at this time. She told us she was a school teacher from 1948. The only way a teacher from that year could have ended up in this time is if they had switched somehow, but we have no way of knowing with any certainty. We found the yearbooks from the school, census records, etc., and verified that Miss Lake was indeed from 1948. She, too, hated her life and hated her world and dreamed of a different life."

" Am I supposed to find this other woman?" I laughed. "You want me to time travel?"

"We don't know for certain, but we want you to try. We want you to focus on the specifics of a time, and as you remove yourself from this time, you will try to control the time you choose. Once you are there, if you make it, give evidence of your existence, which will exist in the historical record so that we can track you. Use your name, or pick a new one. We don't know if our subject went to 1948 or ceased to exist, leaving a gap. We spent a year searching for evidence from her that year, and so far, nothing has come up. But to answer your question, your goal is not to find anyone; there is no espionage or intrigue. Just make a life the best you can."

"You are asking me to risk my life."

"Exactly," he continued. "Because it sounded to us as if you have no attachment to this life and might be willing."

"How do you know I won't go to the press and expose this

whole scam?"

Mrs Miles smiled. "Feel free, they would think you are fucking crazy. Go tell them an agency that does not exist wants you to time travel and see if you're not locked up." She was cold-blooded; I liked that in a woman.

"Can I think about it?"

"Of course, you can; we will stay in town for a few days; we are at the Marriott in St. Paul; just let us know when you have decided." I said nothing, but that was the hotel I worked at, and I don't think it was a coincidence.

Chapter 3

Two days later, I was sitting with my dick in my hand, watching some crap on Porn Hub, when I realised the decision had already been made. What the fuck, why not?. I cleaned up, called Mrs. Miles's room and then quit my job without notice. Work, gym, whiskey, porn hub. What did I have to live for?

I wrote a will. If I had not surfaced a year from August 11, 2001, my apartment and all my possessions would go to Akasha Johnson. She was a hotel maid who had nothing but a smile. She worked hard, never complained, and had little to show. It's funny. I first felt terrific about my life when preparing to leave it. I packed some clothes and met Mrs Miles and Mr Kimball at the airport. They took me to a part of the airport I did not recognise. We were flying in a private jet owned by the state department. I felt positively optimistic for the first time in my life. At first, it was small talk, mostly bullshit, but as we settled in and were given water. Then, the conversation began for real.

Mrs Miles wore a dress that did not try to hide her assets, and it offered me a focus point as we talked. Her voice was still cold and businesslike. "If there were a year you could go to, what year would it be?"

"1945" I had no hesitation in saying this. I had already thought about it.

"Why?"

"I want to live for a while in a time when the world had hope, not like today. I like to experience life disconnected. No cell phone or computer, the war was over, and the world was giddy about starting a new life.

"And what if you cease to exist?"

"No harm, no foul. I won't be conscious of no longer existing and can't sue, so you have no worries. Life's ending does not scare me. Life going on the way I live it does."

"And what if you end up in another time or another country? What if our experiment fails?"

"Then I make the best of it, and you gotta realise it is going to be a fucking adventure. If I end up as a caveman, I learn to hunt; another time I learn to farm, in the 1920s, I invest in gold. Whatever it is, it will be a wild ride. I won't be bored; I will never be bored."

Mr. Kimball picked up the phone. "1945" is all he said, and then we were served meals. I had skipped breakfast, so the grub was welcome. Best aeroplane food I had ever tasted.

We arrived in D.C. "There will be a car, Mr Olaysiz, that will take you to your hotel while we prepare an apartment for you."

"Hey, Mrs. Miles, how about you call me John, and I call you?"

"You call me Mrs Miles. If 1945 is where you are headed, you must learn to be more formal. You might also choose a name for your new life that is a little less 'ethnic.'"

"You are not wrong. Is John Evans generic enough?"

"John Evans is perfect. Order from room service this evening, and we will see you in the morning, Mr. Evans. A car will come, and the driver will bring you to our workspace."

I shook hands with Kimball and Miles and got into the car. I was whisked off to the Waldorf Astoria, the nicest hotel I had ever been in. I didn't just have a room; I had a suite. The television had been removed. In its place was a stack of books. I spotted 'Towards Zero', an Agatha Christie book I had never read, so I made myself at home and started in. The title seemed appropriate.

At some point, I set the book down and fell asleep. It was after 9. I called down to room service. I couldn't help but notice the dial phone.

"Mr. Evans, allow me to review your menu tonight; if you have no objection, you will be served a seafood cocktail followed by a Filet of Beef with string beans and potatoes au gratin. Dessert will be a Raspberry Vanilla Glace along with petit fours and coffee. We will also bring up a decanted bottle of Pinot Noir. Will that be acceptable?"

"Make the steak rare, and we've got a deal." I could see they had already begun working on my brain. No TV and a meal that sounded like the greatest culinary hits of the past. When was the last time anyone served a petit four? The decanted wine must mean they did not have an old bottle lying around. In for a penny, in for a pound.

The meal was great, except for the funny little cake cookies. One bite, and I was done. The coffee countered the wine so I could read just long enough to finish the book before sleep. I was at peace with whatever the hell was coming because I slept like a tired kid at the end of a long drive.

Chapter 4

When I woke up, I knew enough to ask them to send breakfast. The room service waiter set up the tray, not waiting for a tip. It must have been included. I had a big pot of black coffee, two soft-boiled eggs, and toast with butter—Spartan, but enough. I enjoyed dipping the toast into the eggs. I was like a kid, playing with my food.

I showered, dressed and went down to look for the car. Within minutes, a 1940 Lincoln Continental Coupe with tinted windows showed up. The driver opened the door "Mr. Evans." I liked the name because it suited me when I had my clothes on. I was driven to a modern office complex and taken to the basement, where a schoolroom had been set up. It was complete with wooden desks and chairs, a blackboard, and a film projector sitting at the back.

Mr. Kimball was waiting. "Mr Evans, would you please go behind this screen, remove all of your clothing and put on the clothes we have made for you? By tomorrow, you will have a new suitcase with several changes of clothes."

There was a choice of underwear, high-waisted tighty whities or trim boxers that buttoned shut. I went with boxers. I was not going to go through the day with little Evans bound and gagged. He needed room. The slim-fit trousers and the button-down shirt fit me well. I slipped on the socks and a pair of Oxfords.

"When we finish today, we have a barber who will remove the beard and give you a proper haircut."

School began in 1912, the new year of my birth, as it were. We were up to 1922 when it was time to break for lunch.

As we sat down, the music started. I recognised Doris Day and The Andrews sisters. Fortunately, my DJ gave the names of the rest of the artists as they played.

A server brought in Sloppy Joes with carrot sticks and an Almond Joy. Mr. Kimball explained that the Almond Joy was introduced in 1945 and was all the rage.

"Good to know." I popped one in my mouth; not bad. The Joe was alright, but a little sweet for me. Funny, I knew both foods existed but had never tried either. I ate all my carrot sticks, and while Perry Como crooned in the background, I learned the story of William of Orange and how carrots got their ubiquitous colour.

When we got to 1923, newspapers came out. "Schools at the time taught current events; these are just the highlights, but you have to be a part of the time you are in, or you could end up in a mental hospital. I read about the polio Epidemic. Fortunately, I was vaccinated.

Every day more years, more highlights, more tests. I always passed. We went forward and back in time; years were shouted out, and I would give the highlights.

As a reward for my hard work, Mr Kimball offered. "I know how important exercise is, so if you like, your driver will take you to a local gym. He will have a gym bag in the trunk for you. I ask that you speak to no one other than your driver, who will accompany you the entire time."

The first stop was the barber. He attacked my beard with a trimmer and then a straight-edge razor. I had not seen my face in a decade, and it had thinned out. I was not bad-looking at all. He then went at my hair with a razor and scissors. The cut was not severe but was parted and combed to the side. The look flattered my face. Then we took off for the gym.

My driver stood and watched me while I changed into the wife beater, shorts and Keds provided. The lockers had no locks, so I was sure we were in the senate gym. It was older and dumpier than I had imagined. I worked out hard and lifted heavy. I was not sure when I would be given another chance. I was not sure about anything. My driver, whom I suspect was guarding me against the world with driving being the ancillary job, stayed with me, spotted me and even got me a towel when I began to perspire. I saw one other guy reading newspapers and walking on a treadmill. When you walk slowly enough to read, it is not a workout.

After almost two hours, I hit the shower. There were eight heads, with no privacy but the modern amenity of soap dispensers. It's good that I'm not shy, as my driver stood there watching. The doughy, shapeless guy from the treadmill came into the shower and extended his hand. "John Edwards."

"John Evans." and we laughed—my first naked handshake.

"How long have you been on the hill," he asked.

"I'm just a guest." I quickly rinsed and dried off before the conversation got too chummy. I would not want my driver to give me a cross-look.

I felt immeasurably better and was back in my room by 8. I called room service and told them to bring up whatever was on the menu.

Along with the decanted wine and iceberg lettuce salad was duck l'orange, a dish I had heard of but never tasted. I loved it.

When the waiter dropped off my meal, he said he would return with the dessert and coffee. He looked offended when I told him coffee only and assured me that I had to try the dessert, promising it had been made with very dark chocolate and would not be too sweet. I figured I could chop it and flush it down the toilet to make him happy.

He arrived with a small white mound over which he poured flaming brandy. I took a bite, and inside was a very dark chocolate ice cream, Baked Alaska, another dish I had never tried. I enjoyed the novelty of it, but I only ate half. I was going to have to tell my handlers to cut the sugar. I was not going to get fat on their watch.

I turned to the books and began to go through the titles. This was a world I could live in. I had always liked reading, but the damn idiot box was too distracting and compelling to resist entirely.

Mr. Kimball was to be my teacher, at least for the historical portion. I wore yesterday's clothes as my bag had disappeared. All of my toiletries had been replicated with models from yesteryear.

Breakfast was the same, with the addition of some fresh fruit.

Soon, we had caught up to 1940. Great Britain was introducing food rationing. I knew the US also did it. I hoped reading about it was enough, and I am not sure I could handle it if they made me eat Spam.

We were just getting the highlights. The details of life would come once we got to 1945.

At the end of the day, we brought the projector out from the corner, set up a portable screen, and watched Snow White and the Seven Dwarfs, the Disney version. It was a film I was sure to have seen. I liked it and decided I must have had a happy childhood.

For the next twenty-one days, weekends included, this became my routine; some new clothes were introduced, and the ones I was wearing were laundered. We went back to the beginning and then jumped around. He was forcing my mind to keep things in order and context.

As I learned the history of the world, I started to think of it as my current events, and then they moved me into my apartment.

It was a one-bedroom in the Cairo apartment complex. The building was built in the 1800s, but the apartment was 1945 modern. It was a trip to see. The kitchen was white with yellow tiles on the counter and yellow curtains. The refrigerator and freezer were stocked with food. I was going to miss room service. The sofa was skinny but comfortable enough. Each morning, a Times was delivered as if it were on that day in 1945: books, magazines, every detail thought of. The 'office' had been equipped with even a home gym, primitive but with enough weights and a bench to keep my sanity. After I had scrambled my eggs, Mrs. Miles came to my door.

"Today, we will learn how to meditate and break the strings of time that have tethered you here. I must remind you again that anything can happen at any time during this process. Nothing from the modern world will be transported; all of it will be left behind. Do I have your consent to proceed?"

"I am ready to stop playing let's pretend. Get on with it."

"Take off your shoes and sit comfortably on the floor with your legs crossed in the lotus position. This was not a natural way to sit for me. I had tight hips and had to ease into it. " She walked over to the turntable and put on a record. It was just tones. Low tones varied with drumming. "Now, just focus on your breath. Be in your chosen world in that decade and just breathe." I did as instructed. Unwanted thoughts crept into my head, but I stayed with it until the record ended.

"How are you feeling?"

"It's been a little lonely, but those weights will help me work off some steam."

"We can't introduce anyone else into this world we have created. Can you cope?"

"I can cope."

"Good. Tomorrow I will be back, and we will go for longer.
"

And we did, day after day, week after week; we meditated, and I lived in partial isolation. I was living only for the moments when one of them would come over, and I had some company.

This went on for some time. It was not a bad life, but I was still in the year 2000.

Chapter 5

The paper that morning was from November 11, 1945.

As I read the paper, I waited for my visit. When I answered the door, Mr. Kimball and Mrs. Miles stood there.

I made coffee, and we sat down; Kimball began. "We have come to the point where we may have to admit this experiment is either not working, or we are unable to replicate our previous results. Something is tethering you to this time; something you love or want keeps you here. We can assist and send you anywhere you like, new documents, new life. We will make the best of this situation."

I sat and thought for a hard minute. "It's you; you are what is keeping me here. Mrs Miles, you are the only company I have been getting and living in isolation sucks. Your daily visits are what keep me going. This may seem crazy, but I want you both to stand outside in the hall. Give me an hour by myself to go through the meditation. Your other subject slipped away in the night when you were not present. Let me try. If I fail, we'll talk about the options.

Looking completely unconvinced, Mrs Miles responded..."Sure, of course. We'll go outside.

I put on the record and wiped my mind of everything, including the mugs in the hallway. I started to feel myself slipping as if I were moving. I glanced at the clock above the mirror—11:11 a.m. I closed my eyes and sank further as if I were going through a black tunnel and could see a light at the end. Go into the light. Maybe this was death, but I stayed with the feelings and the visions and the next thing I knew, I was sitting on a marble floor and feeling water pouring down my back.

I stood up, trying to orient myself. I was naked as the day I was born, standing under a shower in a marble stall; on the shelf was a bar of soap and a clean towel. I decided to stay put and try to understand where I was. I listened to the voices, all men.

"I'm going to head to the pool."

"I need a haircut so badly, but it's Sunday, dammit. I am going to have to use my lunch hour tomorrow."

"Barber is out on Monday; you have to wait til Tuesday."

"Damn."

"So where is Mitch? I haven't seen him for a week."

"You know he is going to marry old Judge Sprizzo's daughter. The family invited him on the Queen Elizabeth; they are cruising to Europe and won't return until after Christmas."

"My gosh, that family has got money."

"Don't they, though."

There was a cadence to the speech as if I were listening to a Tennesee Williams play. I could not place the accent. I turned off the water and dried myself; only then did I realise the water was also coming from my eyes. I took a few deep breaths, dried my face and, wearing only a towel, stepped out into this new world.

I have been in many locker rooms, but this was a sausage party like I had never seen. I went to look at the pool; everyone was swimming naked. We had not covered men's clubs in my history classes.

There were big wooden lockers but no locks. I opened an empty one and feigned outrage.

"Everything is gone."

The attendant came over immediately. "Are you sure you used this locker, sir?"

"I am sure, locker number 8. I just arrived in town this morning. I am a friend of the Sprizzo family, and the judge told me to use his member privilege since they were out of town. And now everything I own is gone."

"Take a seat, sir; I will take care of this. "

I noticed the attendant and the cleaning person were the only black faces in the crowd, and they both went to the men, asking them to check their lockers. They were certain it was a mistake on my part. Finally, the attendant approached me. "The manager does not work on Sunday, but he is coming in, and we have called the police. I am going to need your sizes, sir. Of course, it being Sunday, everything is closed, but the manager of D.H. Holmes is here today, and he will go over and get you something to wear."

A few minutes later, a very harried man approached me. "I am Michael Laurine, the manager of this club, and I want to assure you that in all of our history, nothing like this has ever happened. The police are downstairs, and I will file a report; I just need to know what you had in your locker, as tomorrow I will be dealing with the insurance company. "

I had seen the Times-Picayune on the table in front of me and did some quick calculations. I was in New Orleans, and rent was 40 bucks a month on the high end. $2,000 would stake me for a year if I needed to take a while to reinvent.

"I am afraid, sir, everything I own was in that locker. I took the train down from Chicago. I am friendly with the Sprizzo family, which is why I chose New Orleans. After a family tragedy, I needed a fresh start, so I had a bag with my clothes and $2,500 in cash in my wallet. I have no identification or other documents and no idea what I am going to do at this point. " That much was true, but the rest I made up as I went along.

He gasped at the amount but kept his composure. "Your clothes should be here momentarily, and I will deal with the police so as not to trouble you. Sunday, we are on the honour system here, and someone without honour made his way into the club, and we will take full responsibility.

A few minutes later, the store manager approached. "Jim Mitchell, I am pleased to make your acquaintance, even under such unfortunate circumstances. If you will get dressed, you can advise me if anything is ill-fitting, and I will exchange it for you; the store is very close."

"Thank you so much, Mr Mitchell. I am John Evans, and you can be sure I will be a loyal customer in the future."

"Think nothing of it."

I got dressed, and everything fit beautifully. Wondering what my next step would be, Mr. Laurine came to me. "If you will permit me, sir, I would like to take you to lunch, and then you are welcome to stay with me until the insurance is sorted unless you have another friend you can call on."

"I welcome your hospitality, sir."

As we left the locker room, we passed the naked swimmers and made our way downstairs. In addition to the workout equipment, they had a bar, library, barber shop, and restaurant closed on Sundays. "As Judge Sprizzo's guest, I will add your name to our roster, and you will have full club privileges for the next year, even after the Judge has returned. It is the least we can do under such circumstances." I could see I was going to have to get to this Sprizzo guy the moment he returned. Either that or leave town.

As we walked, I tried to keep my sanity and notice everything. Mr. Laurine chattered nervously, and I made enough proforma responses to keep him talking. We arrived at the Clover Grill.

"This is a new restaurant for New Orleans. It has only been here six years, but you can get breakfast if you like, or the burger is quite good here. We sat at a Formica table and were greeted by a comely waitress.

"Hey darling, you are a new face round here, and I like new faces; what will you have?"

"Two over easy, toast, butter and bacon, and coffee. It's been a stressful morning, and I need to get my head together."

'I will keep your cup full. And you, Michael?"

"A burger will suit me just fine, with fries and a Coca-Cola."

It was hard not to notice the serving sizes when the meal came. The burger and fries were about ⅓ of the size I was used to. No wonder no one was fat. If I have one phobia, it is fat. I consider myself normal-sized, but I was Minnesota skinny.

I was doing my best to stay calm, to stay present, and to be one step ahead of the game. I was internally shocked that I was here and wondered who had been in that shower stall before me and where he was now.

He kept calling me Mr. Evans....."Hey, as long as we are going to be roomies, at least for a few days, call me John."

"I would never presume, but with your permission, I shall. I am Michael, and I want to thank you. You have been most civil about this incident, and I will work hard to ensure it is resolved as quickly as possible."

The bread was just sliced white, but the eggs and the bacon were incredible.

Chapter 6

I didn't feel bad scamming an insurance company. I just needed to stay calm and take it day by day. I made Michael nervous. He prattled on and on about nothing. I could stand it for a few days. Finally, "You have been to New Orleans before, sir?"

"Yes, briefly as part of a trial," I spoke before thinking. Why would I have been here for a trial?

"And that is how you know the judge. What is it you do, sir?"

"I would rather not talk about it, if you don't mind."

"Of course. Did you see much of the city when you were here?"

"I am afraid not; I just got in and out." The truth was that I had been here only for a drunken bachelor party with some co-workers. I had seen nothing but strippers that weekend.

"Then I will take you for a walk. I live uptown, but we can walk through the quarter."

The Quarter had not yet become the domain of drunken frat boys. While there were bars, it seemed civilised. We cut down to Royal Street. Elegant shops and art galleries lined our walk to Canal Street. He talked and talked, pointing out everything. I mostly tuned him out and focused on observing. I needed to fit in, so I had my eyes on everyone. Women looked great in the clothes. A lot of pencil line skirts hugged all the right parts. Even the wide skirts hugged the waist and breasts. It was conservative in a way that showed everything. There were not so many white gloves, but I remembered that it was the late 50s that popularised that look and Breakfast at Tiffany's introduced the long white glove. It was funny to have memories of things that did not yet exist.

I preferred uptown to the quarter and loved being out among people after my time in isolation. Since I was not wearing a watch, I asked Michael the time: 4 p.m., which was okay. I had only been here five hours, and it felt good.

When we got to Michael's house, I smelled family money. It was very nice for a manager, even at such a plush club as New Orleans Athletic. The antiques smelled of old money as we entered. "I must apologise. I turned the second bedroom into a study, but of course, you will take the bed, and I will sleep on the couch."

"I'm not taking your bed; I'll be fine on the couch."

"I insist."

"I refuse." I could see the relief on his face as he allowed me my refusal. No one ever really wants to give up their bed.

"I am afraid we must make do with a bachelor supper. I do make a very nice Salisbury Steak if I say so myself."

"That sounds great, thanks."

"May I offer you a cocktail before I head to the kitchen?"

"Whiskey, if you have it, neat."

"Bourbon or Scotch?"

"Bourbon."

He went into the kitchen, and I sat down and went through the books. Jean Genet's "Our Lady of the Flowers."' Blair Nigel's Strange Brother:" These were not the books most men had casually strewn about. I was getting a sense of my host. New Orleans was a libertine city, and if sexuality was not flaunted, it was not prosecuted. I wasn't going to bring it up, but if he did, it was fine by me.

Ninety minutes later, he shouted that dinner was served. The table was beautifully set, candles lit, wine decanted, and the plates photo-worthy. I now had no doubt regarding my host's proclivities.

"We have an outstanding Bordeaux. Now that the war is over, ships have just begun coming again with French wine. Keeping a cellar in this climate is hard, so I rely on imports. When good wine was scarce, I had to make do with Cabernet from Krug and BV."

"You seem young to be the manager of such an exclusive club."

"You flatter me, sir. I am 43 years of age."

I had not intended to flatter him, but he did not look a day over 30. I thought he was younger than me. I am the type to have a 5 o'clock shadow by noon. He was very slim with pale, refined features and blond hair.

The conversation was pleasant. He was no longer so nervous, and the prattling had ended. After enough wine, he mustered up the courage.

"I assure you, I will make no untoward moves or solicitations, but I strongly suspect we are of different persuasions."

"I figured that out from the books, no problem for me. Have you got a boyfriend?"

He blushed again. "There is a gentleman with whom I spend time on occasion; unfortunately, due to societal pressure, he has a wife. Only those of us who have family and a certain amount of security can afford the luxury of being a confirmed bachelor."

"Like Rock Hudson and Tab Hunter."

"I am not familiar with Mr. Hudson or Mr. Hunter. Do they live in New Orleans?"

I was going to have to be more careful; those two were a few years ahead.

"They are a couple of young actors trying to catch a break."

"How do you come up with such information?"

"Friends in the business. Hey, I guarantee you the world will come around. Most of it, anyway."

"It is good to have such optimism."

"Just call me a cockeyed optimist."

"What a charming phrase."

I took a breath; I had jumped ahead by four years with that reference. I needed to get my head together.

"I know a few folks in New York; one is working on a musical, and that is a song title if they manage to get it produced."

Once the topic turned to musicals, I lit a fire in my host, who now saw me as a friend and ally. A second bottle of wine was opened, and I got the play-by-play of Carmen Jones, Oklahoma, and Carousel. I was a good guest and did not tune out; his enthusiasm for the topic made the stories worthwhile.

I was grateful when he went upstairs and brought down linens to make up the couch. With the mind-blowing excitement of the day, I did not know if I would sleep, but the whisky and wine did their number, and I was out.

Chapter 7

I smelled coffee and dressed, folding the sheets carefully before heading to the dining room.

There was a fruit salad with fresh mint from the garden. Winter in New Orleans is like spring in Minnesota, with cool days and warm days but rarely a freeze. I could get used to this.

"How do you take your coffee?"

"Black."

"No milk? I have warmed it."

"Black. Not anything."

"Chicago is a different world. I must go to work today and take care of your insurance claim, but this afternoon, I will be at your disposal to help you take care of getting identification."

"My license was from Illinois."

"Clarice over at the DMV is my cousin; we'll go see her if anyone can find a way she can."

He had left his car at the Athletic Club yesterday to babysit me, so we walked. He showed me where the library was on St. Charles and instructed me to get to the club via streetcar. He handed me a few coins for the fare. I honestly was relying on the kindness of strangers.

At the library, I had the librarian pull everything she had about Chicago. I had to learn that city to deal with any questions that might come up. I got enough general information to create the lies needed.

I was at the club a little after noon. Michael informed his assistant and the receptionist that he would help the victim of yesterday's unfortunate incident, and off we went.

We walked to his 1942 Hudson Commodore in the parking lot. This was, without a doubt, the most fantastic car I had ever seen. He drove a stick shift, but I remembered the invention of the automatic in one of my classes, so I knew it existed at this time.

We drove to the DMV, where his cousin Clarice asked me to fill out a form with my height, weight, etc., while she called.

"To whom am I speaking? .....Doris, this is Clarice from the New Orleans DMV. Can you check your files for a John Evans? His license was stolen."

I stopped writing after my name and listened carefully while I pretended to stare at the paper on my clipboard. As she made notes, I listened: "1225 North Wells, born July 7, 1912. You remember his renewal...oh, is he really? Oh my goodness."

I handed over the paper with the correct name and former address. She smiled at me as she wrote out my license. They were still paper with no photo, which suited me just fine. "You did not tell us you were a private detective. Doris remembered you from your license renewal."

Micheal gave me a look of understanding. "That's how you know, Judge Sprizzo, it must have been some case if you can't talk about it."

I thought fast and turned to Doris. "That's another license I need to replace. Do you know if Louisiana has reciprocity with Illinois for professional licenses?"

"Let me call Harvey and find out. I don't think it is a state but a city license." She picked up the phone. "Harv, did you hear about that poor young man who lost everything at the Athletic club yesterday? He's sitting right here. Doris over at the DMV in Chicago verified his credentials. Do we have reciprocity with Illinois? Chicago, so it is a city license. If I send him over, can you take care of it along with his carry permit? You are a doll; Michael will fetch him right over."

That required a passport photo printed on thin paper, so we stopped and had the photos done. I figured I should get a passport as long as I was on a lucky streak.

Harv was a doll. I had never shot a gun, but I now had a profession and a permit to carry. Both licenses had my photo.

A stop at the post office, and I filled out the passport application. My heart stopped short when she asked for a birth certificate. Michael came to my rescue.

"He just moved down from Chicago and lost everything; his birth certificate was likely in his bag with his other papers."

"I have to have 6 points of ID. What do you have?"

I laid it all out in front of her, my heart racing. She looked, and I waited. "Okay, I will sign off on it. It takes about six weeks to arrive, and it will go to Michael's house since you don't have an address yet."

"Why don't you come back to the gym with me? While you work out, I will have Nadine add your shirt and underthings to the wash. I don't have shoes to lend..."

"I'll swim, no costume needed."

We walked to the club and went in.

Michael, after yesterday, would you mind keeping my documents in your desk down here."

"Absolutely. I will call and have the attendant stand by and bring your things to the laundry."

I got undressed, rinsed off and dove into the pool. I have got to admit swimming naked felt very good. I was never a fan of that clingy fabric, and I liked the freedom of no modesty whatsoever. I was new here, and people looked at me curiously, but most looked at my face. Only about half the men were circumcised, so maybe they feared I was Jewish. Once I had some coin, I would buy a cross or something to wear. Anti everything sentiment was still strong in the time I had chosen.

After a long, long swim, I hit the sauna. It was huge, with both the wooden benches I was used to and actual wooden lounge chairs. My presence stopped the conversation as the three men wanted to know all about me.

"I am Giles, and I heard about the unfortunate incident yesterday. Is there anything I can do?"

"Mr Laurine has offered me hospitality until the matter is settled."

"Of course he has; he is a fine Gentleman from a good family."

Falwell and Leo also introduced themselves. I guess when you are dick-forward, you can be on a first-name basis.

"Now, what is it you do up in Chicago?"

"Private Detective."

That got their attention. Falwell leaned forward. "Are you setting up here in New Orleans?"

"I will be."

"I am the president over at Whitney Bank, and there are occasions when I or some of my associates might need your services. Once you are established, be sure to make a call."

"You will see me before that; I will need a bank account."

"Consider it done. I will use Michael's address until you get your own place, and you come to see me once the insurance settles."

'Thank you, I will."

He didn't ask for a Social Security number. I would have to see what I could do about getting one for when it was needed. I knew not everyone at this time had one, but the day would soon come when it was required.

Leo was a doctor, and Giles was a lawyer. I would definitely make a call on Giles 'once I was established.'

"Evans is a Welsh name, isn't it?"

"Yes, Leo, but I take after my mother's side of the family; she was a Mistretta, Italian Catholic."

And the final barriers dropped. I had lied my way into this world and had acceptance. If I had ever loved my father, I would feel guilty about abandoning my heritage, but he was an abusive asshole. After my mother left him, she bought a handgun, and when he found us, she shot him and then herself, dumping me on my own at 17. At least she had kept a savings account, or I would have been out on the street.

I was determined to navigate the world I found myself in because I had no fondness for the one left behind.

After my shower, my clean and dry underwear, socks, and newly pressed shirt were all waiting on a hanger. Michael would not take money, but I would find a way to repay him.

After another expertly prepared bachelor meal, I began reading Jean Genet. I had a start when the drag queen in the novel was named Divine. I wondered if this was the inspiration for the 70s trash star Divine. Several chapters in, and it was time for sleep.

Chapter 8

Michael was running late the following day, so I suggested we skip breakfast, and I would be happy to have black coffee. He worried I was not eating enough, and I feared that I was eating too much and too well, even with the smaller portions. He told me to pick up the phone if it rang. The day was warm, so I settled in the garden to read. After about 4 hours, I was lost in the story when I heard the shrill shriek of the telephone. I went in to answer it.

It was Michael. "If you can make your way down here, the adjustor just dropped off your check, and there is still time to get it to the bank."

I took the streetcar as far as Canal Street and finished on foot. I got inside, and after the greetings, I was handed an envelope. The check was for $5,000.00 US dollars. This was about double the average professional yearly salary at the time. "I didn't lose this much."

"I put in the claim for more; you have to replace your clothes, and the loss of the documents and the time spent is worth something. Besides, that is what insurance is for. We have been paying these vultures for decades without a claim, and they are not likely to question me."

"Thank you."

"And don't feel rushed. You are a welcome guest as long as it takes for you to find a place to live.

I went to the bank and deposited it into the account which had already been opened for me. I took $100 in cash. I liked cash; it felt good, real somehow. Even when I lived in the debit card world, I always carried cash. I began to walk to try to find an office and a place to live. I wandered the quarter looking for rent signs and saw a few rooms, none suitable. On South Peters, there was a sign with a telephone number. It was a single house, very narrow, like ½ of a double that had been lopped off. It was close enough to the business district to get the business trade. I was beginning to think of myself as what I had created myself to be. I was no longer pulling off a con. I was committing to a new life. I found a phone booth and called the number.

The landlord had an office nearby and agreed to meet. I waited. Fifteen minutes later, he showed up. Micha Goldstein shook my hand and then took me inside. The house was shotgun-style, with four rooms connected. The kitchen was at the back, then what could be a living/dining area, bedroom with a full bath, and the front room with a half bath could be used as an office. I asked about the zoning.

"This was Doc Schuler's place 'til he retired. I tried to sell it for a few months, but no buyers, even though it is mixed zoning. You see, Doc Schuler took care of a lot of women who did not want to be in the family way, and people think the remains are buried in the yard out back. They believe the place to be haunted.

"I only believe in ghosts I can see. How much do you want for the place?"

"Five thousand, which I think is only fair. After Doc left, I put a lot of money into adding a kitchen. That kitchen has an electric refrigerator. It is very modern; you save the cost of ice delivery. Doc put in the second bathroom right off the front room for patients. Not many places around here have a second bathroom."

I took a walk-through. Spartan, but it was nice. It had wood floors, solid construction and a great kitchen with a double oven. I would have to learn how to make more than scrambled eggs.

"1,000 down, cash if you want, and you carry the note. Give me a good interest rate, and I will give you 200 a month, no prepayment penalty."

"Why not go to the bank for the note?"

"I don't like banks, and banks don't like me. What would rent be?" The truth is that Fallwell would probably give me the loan, but I hate paperwork.

"$55.00 a month."

"Even if you throw me out and have to take it back, you have a grand in your pocket that would cover the rent and more."

We made the deal, walked to the bank, signed, and I gave him cash. I hope the tax man never saw a dime.

Before Roe v. Wade, most towns had a doctor like him if you knew who to ask. I wasn't worried about being haunted.

Chapter 9

I got back uptown right after Michael. I gave him the news. "I must make a celebratory dinner to properly welcome you, my homeowner friend."

I insisted on taking him out to dinner to thank him for all he had done. After the obligatory protests, he agreed.

We went to Commander's Palace, and they welcomed him as an old friend. We got the corner table upstairs facing the garden. I let him order for both of us and had my first taste of Turtle soup. Then redfish stuffed with crawfish and a brown butter sauce, all with a great bottle of imported French wine. The whole thing set me back $5.00. I had to start to realise the value of a buck in the time I was living in. I was happy to pay it. This man had upped my claim to the point where I could buy a house.

The next day I went shopping. First Stop DH Holmes, and as promised, I was a loyal customer. I made sure to say hello to Mr Mitchell. I purchased two suits, the under-suit essentials, two pairs of shoes, some Keds for the gym, a pair of shorts, and a wifebeater. I took it to my new home and stuck it in what would be the bedroom. The house had no closets, so I tied up a clothesline that could handle a few hangers for the moment.

I found a furniture store and got a bed, a double. I was optimistic—this, along with a desk, two chairs, a sofa and a filing cabinet for the office. I had business cards printed on a hand-run press. I hung up a shingle I had ineptly painted and returned to Michael's as the bed was not to be delivered until the next day.

I purchased nothing for the kitchen; I would be eating out for a few days.

Michael prepared his version of a celebratory dinner for my last night on the sofa. He had roasted a golden-skinned chicken, cabbage, carrots and a pot of rice. He served a white Bordeaux alongside. I was going to have to lay in some wine. I was getting used to this.

It's funny how the brain works. It had only been days, but I was starting to become him, me, who I pretended to be. I had memories of the future, but much of the time, I was firmly in the present. This was my life, and I had been right. I was not bored.

After dinner, we talked for a while, and then I finished the book. I started out pulling a con and ended up with a friend. He trusted me, and I was determined to live up to that.

By late Saturday, only six days after I had arrived, I was moved in. There were linens on the bed, wine in the kitchen, one pan and a spatula, and a professional-looking office. I ordered a phone, but it would be over a month before they installed it. I wore a suit, thinking I might treat myself to a nice meal; as I walked back to the front of the house, I heard the door. I had a visitor.

She had blue eyes as cold as ice and a dark blue suit that had been built for her, or she had been created for it. She was a Platinum blonde, with just enough slit on her pencil skirt to move and make me want more. I greeted her, and her name was Mrs. La Branche.

"Sit down and tell me what I can do for you."

"It's my husband; I think he may have been cheating."

"Any man who would cheat on you must be blind."

"He's not blind. Yesterday evening, my husband was shot in the leg. He's fine, but the man he was with was killed."

"You want me to investigate a murder?"

"I don't care about the murder, but yes, do look into it. I want you to investigate the man. I want to know if they were lovers."

"You think your husband may be...."

"I know he is, and I knew he was when he married me. We had an arrangement; he could see who he liked, but never more than twice. He was never to take a lover, never to embarrass me in public."

"What was the name of the victim?"

"Lieutenant Simon Potts."

"I gotta ask, why would you marry a man who...."

"It's a long story."

"I have time."

"The bottom line is money, he came from it, a lot of it. My family is from the wrong side of the tracks. Girls from the Bywater don't marry uptown men. My family had a small grocery store with a sandwich counter, and the boys from his school came by for the catfish po boy. My father fished it fresh every day. We were friendly, and I may have been the only woman he really got to know. When he went to Tulane, there was an incident at the Y.M.C.A. in the steam room. The attendant claimed he saw an encounter, not just boys being boys, but one that required more commitment. When the cops came, he said I was his girlfriend. When they called me in, I vouched for him. I like the sensitive types. The attendant was a black man. He got fired for telling lies about a good citizen. I felt bad about that, so we hired him at the grocery store."

"So you do have a heart?"

"Of course, I have a heart; I just keep it in check. Anyway, after we went shopping for suitable clothes and a new hairstyle, I joined his family for Sunday dinner. And despite the objections due to my background, we married upon his graduation. After a few years, my parents sold the store, and with my help, they could retire comfortably. The arrangement works; I find what I need, and he can keep his job at the law firm. "

"So the murdered guy, tell me about him and why you think they were involved?"

"He was a military officer; they were friends, publicly. Every time he was in town, he came to dinner. Brian, my husband, always walked him back to his hotel and was gone for at least an hour, a nightcap, he told me. Recently, Brian told me that his friend Simon was leaving active service and joining recruiting. Many older officers do this, and he was in his 40s. But then Simon announced he would be permanently stationed in New Orleans. He arrived in town three days ago, and they were inseparable for the first day; that night, he was killed, and Brian was shot in the leg. And it was outside the Bourbon coffee house, a known meeting place for men who prefer the company of other men."

"I'll take the case; my rate is 50 bucks a day with five days paid in advance. I'll take a check. I will begin in the morning."

She wrote the check and her number on a piece of paper. "Keep in touch."

She walked out slowly. She knew the effect she was having. It was 10 minutes before I could stand up in this tight suit.

Three times that night, I woke up in a cold sweat. At 8:45 in the morning, I was standing outside the library. The only books I could find were fiction, so I began to read fictional detective stories. There was a logic to them, a beginning point and always a resolution. They were fast reads. I got a catfish po boy at a grocery in the French Quarter and sat at my desk with my novels, looking for inspiration to pull this gig off. I was determined to earn my money. She hadn't even flinched when I mentioned the amount, which I found out later was much more than double what most Detectives charged at the time.

The next day, I began in earnest. I started at the Bourbon coffee house. It opened at 10 a.m. I arrived at 11. , It wasn't packed, but there were a respectable number of guests, all men. It was apparent they weren't just taking a walk on the wild side; these men lived on the wild side. Pretty soon, I was approached by a guy asking if he could share my table. "Sure."

He sat down. "You don't look like most of the men in here. Are you, by any chance, the lawyer who is going to help the men put together the Steamboat club?"

"What's the Steamboat Club?"

"Nothing yet. It has to be incorporated first, but it will be a crew."

"They are going to be the crew of a steamboat?"

"Not a crew a Krewe...K. R.E.W.E. An officially recognised organisation for Mardi Gras."

"No, I'm not a lawyer...I'm a private dick."

"I love trade, and you are speaking my language."

"It's my career, my job."

"Oh, it seems you were not speaking my language. I think you might be in the wrong place. Men meet and form friendships here; close friendships."

"I'm in the right place. I am looking into the murder of the Navy officer shot right outside a few nights ago."

"I wasn't here that night."

"But you've heard something."

"This town is fueled by gossip. Of course, I have heard something."

He went over and grabbed a paper. I had yet to read it this morning.

Right there on the front page was Mrs La Branche announcing that she had hired a private detective and would not rest until they found the man who had shot her husband—no mention of my name.

The lady had gone public. I wondered what that was about. "So tell me what you have heard?."

"I heard that Mr. La Branche had a crush on that officer."

"So the officer was like you? A gentleman's gentleman?"

"No one knows, and that's the truth. He just brought him here the one time. After about 10 minutes, Brian used the phone booth. They continued talking for about 30 minutes, stepped outside, and he was shot dead, and dead men tell no tales."

"Is this place open late?"

"Until midnight, in the evening. The coffee turns Irish, and the crowd gets happy. They may not have a licence for the Bourbon, as the bartender keeps it under the counter, and you pay for it with tips. Tips that are not put in the register."

"Same guy every night?"

"They are closed Monday and Tuesday."

"So, where do you gather on those days."

"Even we need a day of rest."

"What do you do that lets you be here in the middle of the day?"

"Overnight room service at a hotel. I leave at 8 when the day crew comes in. It is not so busy at night, and I can often get some pretty large tips taking care of the needs of travelling businessmen; they are mostly trade, but I like that."

"I remember."

I gave him my card. "If you hear anything else, let me know."

"You have no telephone number."

"I have no telephone; stop by; the door is open when I am in the office."

I looked at my stack of books: Ellery Queen, Erle Stanley Gardner, Rex Stout, Raymond Chandler, James M. Cain and Dashiell Hammet.

I picked up Mildred Pierce. I knew it as a Joan Crawford star vehicle and wanted to see the story the way Cain intended it. Maybe it would teach me something about the female brain. Maybe not.

I read all afternoon and returned to the coffee house to check out the evening crowd. There was a scattering of wedding rings, but it was just coffee, right? Save its reputation; anyone could have a reason for going there.

I stood at the bar. "Coffee, make it Irish if you can."

"Sugar or milk?"

"Black, I think you're sweet enough."

"I'm not on the menu."

"I just want conversation. I'm trying to fit in, and it seems I am failing. The naval officer who was killed leaving this place, had you ever seen him before?"

"No one had. It was his first time here. I think he was a little uncomfortable with the whole scene. We get an occasional stranger who just wants coffee, But most of the men here know the score.."

"How did he seem to you? Was it just this place that jarred him, or was it the idea of men with men he found distasteful?"

"There is no way for me to know. They got their coffee, sat down, and talked for 10 minutes, really quietly. Then Mr La Branche made a phone call; another 20 minutes passed, and they got up and left. Two shots. A couple of witnesses saw the shooter, a short guy, all in black. The trousers didn't fit. He wore a hat. One odd thing they mentioned. The shoes looked like slippers. The man had the gun in one hand and a bag from DH Holmes in the other. He turned the corner, and 5 minutes later, there was no trace of the guy. He was a good shot, no hesitation."

"Did the witnesses chase him?"

"Do you see anyone in here that you think would chase a man with a gun?"

"Point taken."

"You know the names of the guys?"

"Nigel and Ettienne they got an antique shop on Royal. Roommates, if you get my drift."

I hung around for a couple of hours talking to the men and got nothing helpful. I stopped at Clover for a burger. They had no wine, and I was disappointed. I went home and read for a while and had horrible dreams.

I dreamt I was slipping back to the future, taking inventory of the dry goods at the hotel. I saw Kimball and Miles, and I wanted to get away. I could not escape the monotony of life, and then I woke. I had soaked the bed and was covered in a cold sweat. Buck naked, I got up, figuring I would spend the rest of the night on the couch in the office. I brought the pillow; I would turn it over and use the dry side. Bright light was coming in my front windows, and I panicked that the tunnel of light had come for me.

I took a breath and realised it was car headlights. I saw a figure all in black, so I ducked just as a bullet came through the window. The shooter drove away. I was going to have to get some curtains.

I used the pillow to cushion myself from the broken glass, put on some shorts and made coffee. Sleep was out of the question.

Once the sun was up, I cleaned up the glass and taped the window with bags and boxes.

At 6 a.m., I went to the gym; it was just opening, but I needed to relieve some stress. I worked out hard and lifted heavy. I was trying to force my mind back into my body. I'd never been shot at before.

It was 9 when I was ready to leave. Michael had just come in. I went over to his desk. "It's good to see you, bud. Is there any chance you know a guy who can replace some glass? My front window was broken last night."

"What happened? Are you alright?"

"I am fine. There are probably some kids with rocks. The place is supposed to be haunted. It's the kind of thing kids do."

"Juvenile delinquents. I will call Buddy over at the hardware store; give me a minute." He got on the phone, and it was all arranged quickly. "You head home, and Buddy will meet you there and take care of the windows. The sizes of these shotgun houses are standard; he has glass to fit, and you need to buy some curtains."

"I will take care of that today. And thanks, I appreciate it."

I knew it wasn't kids with rocks. It was someone trying to scare me. Who and why...no idea.

After Buddy installed the window, he gave me a ride to the hardware store. The next store was a housewares store, which gave me an idea. I bought curtain rods, brackets and shower curtain clips. At the housewares store, I found tablecloths that were all cotton. I looked through the stacks until I came across dark red tablecloths. As long as the house was haunted, I would make it look haunted. Standing on a chair, with the help of a screwdriver, I got the brackets hung. The desk was dark brown, the sofa brown leather and the splash of colour was lovely. It also reduced the chances of being seen and shot.

All I knew so far was that this case was dangerous and complicated. Beyond that, I knew nothing. I decided to chat with Nigel and Ettiene. I asked around and got the address of their antique shop in Royal. It was a short walk, and I would need some chow soon anyway.

I went in. A swarthy man built like a boxer was dusting a table. 'Are you Nigel or Ettiene? "

In a voice deeper than mine, he answered. "Ettiene. What can I help you with?"

"I'm Evans, and I am investigating a murder you just happened to witness."

He recoiled. "I've already spoken to the police."

"And now you're going to speak to me. Tell me everything you remember."

"We didn't see much." in a loud voice, "Nigel." Nigel came out of hiding. He was short with a full face. I was guessing Irish. "We didn't see much, really just a short man who shot the Sergeant in the heart and Brian in the leg."

"How close was he?"

"Close to a block away from where we stood."

"I mean, how close to the victims."

"Oh, very. He walked right up to Sergeant Potts and shot him point blank in the chest. The Sergeant fell on Brian, knocking him over, and then the man shot Brian in the leg."

"You use his first name. How well did you two know Brian?"

Nigel blushed deeply. Ettiene turned toward him. "Go ahead, tell him."

Nigel was shaking at this point. "Before I met Ettiene, Brian and I were friends of an intimate nature, but after our third evening, he told me he would never see me again, at least not in the same way. Brian had a deal with his wife. He would not see a man again if he started liking him. I was starting to fall for him, but he was cold-hearted. After that, the most I got was the kind of hello you would say to someone you have never met. Then Ettiene moved down here from Baton Rouge. I had wanted to start a shop, and we scraped the money together between the two of us. At first, we were just business partners, but as time passed."

"I get it, congratulations. It can be hard to find someone in this crazy world. You won't believe me, but I believe men like you will have the right to marry someday."

Ettiene spoke. "I don't believe you, but knowing we have allies beyond our scope is nice. New Orleans is the most libertine city in the world, yet still, we have unfortunate incidents."

"Why do you think the shooter only killed the one man and left Brian with a flesh wound? Was it jealousy?"

"It may have been. He was close enough to kill Brian easily but aimed for the leg."

I thanked them for their time. It seems the Lieutenant was the target, but I was still unsure about the love angle. I had to let this one stew in my brain for a while.

Chapter 10

I went to a little cafe and had some shrimp etouffee. The sauce was heavenly. I was going to have to find a Chinese joint; I needed my vegetables, and my diet had been less than ideal this past week.

I asked the waitress if she knew a good Chinese place. "They got one out by Metairie." That was not walkable. I was going to need a set of wheels. "You know any good used car lots.?" Metairie again. There was a bus. The driver let me off in front of the lot on Jefferson Highway.

The new cars were a pretty penny, and I had to be cautious until Mrs La Branche's check cleared. I had house payments to make, and I had been spending like a drunken sailor. I found a 1942 Ford Super Deluxe convertible in dark Green. I liked it, so knowing the game, I turned away from the car as the salesman approached.

"I'm Kenny, he stuck out his hand. I decided to be civcivilised enough to shake it.

"I don't think we will get to know each other well enough to be on a first-name basis, Mr.?

"I don't believe in being formal with my customers; we are all friends here. Just call me Kenny or Mr Kenny if it makes you more comfortable. I saw you looking at that Ford."

"Nice colour, but you know what Ford stands for, fix or repair daily."

"That's a good one, but this beauty runs like a charm and has low mileage."

"I know, and it was probably driven by an old lady who took it to church once a week and treated it like her own child."

"I don't know who owned it. It came in on one of my days off, but it only has 60,000 miles, and that's not bad. I'll let you have it for $600."

"New, it was what? 2 grand, and now it is a couple of years old. Do you think I was born yesterday? $300, cash."

"$400, and I would have to get my manager's permission even to do that."

"There is no manager, so before you go in the closet and have a pretend conversation while you play with your dick, I am going to write a check for $325. Either you give me the papers, or I tear up the check, your choice."

He made a big show of calling the bank to make sure the check was good before signing the car over to me.

"You drive a hard bargain, sir, but since we took that car on trade, I accept your terms. I must feed my children."

"I don't see a ring, so I am guessing there are no kids unless you fathered them when you were over in Germany. The back of your neck has a shrapnel scar. The bullet just hit the surface, so you were lucky. When you go home, you are either going to get drunk, visit a brothel, or play with your own dick after a sad sandwich." I was right, too, right. He gave me the keys and turned away. I was cruel, but I hate used car salesmen. They try to pretend they are friends while they pick your pocket.

Following the highway back, I made my way home. South Peters was a narrow block; no houses had a garage, so I had to park my car on the street.

I needed to stop spending money and return to earning the money I had been given in advance.

I drove over to the New Orleans Military Ocean terminal. One man was standing at attention in front of each ship. Three ships, I had no idea which one was the right one. I asked. "Which ship was Lieutenant Simon Potts aboard?"

"This one, sir."

"I am looking into the murder. Can I talk to anyone who knew him?"

"Everyone knew him, sir; I will ask the Lieutenant Commander if he will see you. They served together as enlisted men."

I waited for about 10 minutes. It would have been a good time for a cigarette, but I don't smoke.

He returned. "Permission to board, sir. The Commander will see you."

I got on the vessel, and a man of about 45 came over to greet me. "I am Commander Martin. How can I help you?"

"Detective John Evans, private, and I am looking into the murder of your Lieutenant."

"The police are about to close that one. They said it was just the wrong place, wrong time. He was outside a club where known homosexuals meet, and they assumed he was one. Just an angry shooter who hated those types of men."

"So the Lieutenant was not a case of don't ask, don't tell?"

"I am not sure what you mean."

"Is there any chance Lieutenant Potts was homosexual?"

"No sir, I don't believe so. Many in our ranks are. They keep it private, but everyone knows. Simon was married when we first served, and his whole life was about going ashore to be with his wife."

"What happened to the marriage?"

"Three years ago, there was a car crash. She was seven months along and would have been his first kid. It was late in life for both of them, but it finally happened. She was 35, and he was 40 and jumping with joy. After she was gone, his heart was never in his work, so no one was surprised when he applied to go into recruiting. I figured he would work at that for a while and then retire."

"Did the police tell you he was shot point blank?"

"No, sir."

"The gun was held to his chest. This was murder, not some random incident."

He was starting to look pale.

"Let's go sit down," I suggested.

We got to his quarters, and he poured two Bourbon whiskeys. I kept quiet for a minute and just watched his face. The idea of murder shook him to his core. He looked up from his glass, "Why would anyone murder Potts?"

"That's what I am trying to find out. If Potts wasn't an invert, what was his attitude towards them? Did he enforce the blue discharge?"

" He never took it that far, but there aren't many hiding places on a ship, and when he finds men together, he threatens to write a letter to their mothers if the behaviour continues. Close quarters, no women, things happen. The idea of this becoming public curbed the behaviour. The men found other ways to cope with their urges."

"I am familiar with the other ways. All men are."

He laughed, a sad laugh, not hearty nor genuine.

"Look, Commander Martin. I will stay with this case and return as soon as I learn anything."

"Because of the holidays and all the requested leave, we will be in port at least until January 30th doing maintenance work. I would very much appreciate you sharing anything you discover.

I drove back home. I went to a phone booth and called my client.

"I need to talk to your husband. When can I see him?"

"I was wondering how long it would take you to get around to that. Come by tomorrow morning. I will be at the hairdresser, but the housekeeper can take you to him. Let me give you the address."

"It was on your check."

"Of course."

I got off the phone and walked to the French Market. It had less selection than I was used to, but I got carrots and celery, apples, and oranges. Nutritious fibre that took no effort, I could eat it raw. I also picked up some eggs, bacon and nuts. I had gourmet tastes and bachelor skills. I had already spent a chunk of change and wanted to keep my nest egg in the nest. I had some stocks I wanted to buy. I'd made a mental checklist of companies that would make me rich if I purchased at the right time.

Chapter 11

That night, I finally slept well. No panic, no night sweats. I felt pretty happy about how far I had come in such a short time. It was as if I was meant to be here and do this work.

After a good hour's swim and a 10-minute sauna, during which it became apparent that I was still the gossip of the day, I drove uptown to the La Branche home.

A uniformed housekeeper answered the door. I gave her my name, she went upstairs and came down and told me there would be a 10-minute wait. "Would you like a cup of coffee?"

"Sure, if we can have it in the kitchen and you join me."

"I'm not sure that I can do that, sir."

"And I am sure you can. The lady of the house is out, and the man upstairs needs a little time. Take a load off, and have a cup of coffee with me."

"Well, I suppose it would do no harm."

She put on a percolator, and we sat down.

"Do you have a name?"

"Sylvia."

"Good to meet you, Sylvia; I'm John." I extended my hand, and she shook it limply.

"You are aware I am just a servant in this household."

"I am also aware that you are a human being who works hard and sometimes needs to sit down and have a friendly chat.
"

She relaxed a little. "You are not like most white men."

"I'm from Chicago, Sylvia, and we are a different species." I got a full laugh.

"Did you want to question me about the household? I was told to keep my mouth shut around you."

"No. I want to ask you about you. Are you married, single, divorced? What part of town do you live in? Any kids? Stuff like that."

"I don't know why you are interested, but yes, I am married. My husband works in an auto shop and brings me to work here every day. We have a nine-year-old son, and when he finishes school, he stays with my sister until we get home for the day. We live East in a little neighbourhood by the Lake."

"I am not married. I have been here barely a week and already have a house, car, and business."

A genuine big smile. "I know all about you, Mr. Evans. You are the talk of the town. You do things fast, like a Yankee. You bought the Doc's old place. We all felt sorry because it could not even be rented, and you showed up and bought it outright. There are no ghosts, just a lot of memories. I don't know how many uptown girls had to visit the Doc, but most of them at least once before marriage. And men like him upstairs would go if they got the clap. His leaving left a void in this town. I hear tell there is a Doc up in Baton Rouge who is doing the same for girls in trouble, but that's a long drive."

"I bet you know everyone's secrets."

"You know I do, we all do. There are no secrets in this town, just folks pretending like they don't know to keep being sociable with those who have money. There is one god in New Orleans, and it ain't the Catholic god like folks pretend. It's the greenback."

"How many men like him upstairs are there?"

"Uptown, we got plenty; if you got money, you buy a wife, and she takes care of her business like he takes care of his, and everybody knows everything. You go to the Athletic Club up on North Rampart, right?"

"You know I do."

She chuckled, "Yes, I do, and even that club has an invisible line. One crowd goes in the sauna, and that's the old boys' network. Get in good with them, and you will always have work, even at 50 bucks a day, and then another crowd goes into the steam room. Stick your head in some time, and you will know what I am saying is true. YMCA same story. Men and their business is a tale as old as time."

She glanced at her watch. "You should probably head up now." It was a good reminder I needed both a watch and a calendar. I wasn't even sure what day it was.

Mr La Branche was on crutches dressed only in boxer shorts and a shirt, wife beater style. He spent much time at the Y and outside of the steam room. Like me, his musculature was unfashionable for the time.

"You will have to forgive me, sir, but with this large dressing on my leg, I am unable to properly attire myself. I am here at your command and will answer any question, no matter how intimate. I am aware my wife has already related our arrangement, so I know you will not be shocked."

"Just tell me what you remember about that night."

My friend and I had a conversation over a coffee, stepped out into the night, and a shooter came from around the corner and shot him in the heart. Then I was shot in the leg, and the shooter fled the scene."

"You got up to make a phone call; who did you call?"

For a second or two, his facade slipped. This was not a question he was expecting. I could see the gears turning."

"I called my mother. I had intended to drop by, and there was not going to be any time that evening."

It was a lie, but I could not tell if he was lying about the reason he called or who he called.

"How was the shooter dressed?"

"Black as I recall."

"Hat or gloves?"

"Both, I think."

"Tall or short, fat, muscular, lean?"

"I did not get that good a look."

"Why do you think he only aimed for your leg?"

"I have no way of knowing what was in his mind at the time."

"No, of course not, but doesn't it seem odd that this shooter out of nowhere murdered him and spared you?"

"I don't know what is odd in incidents of this type. It was the first time I was ever shot at."

"So you were not involved in the war, never drafted?"

"I was excused. I am an only son, and my father passed in 1939."

"Sorry to hear that."

"Aren't you going to ask about the nature of my relationship with Simon?"

"Tell me about your relationship with Giles."

I could see his surprise at this question as well.

"We had a few passing but unsatisfactory moments. He was upset because I refused to invest in his antique shop. But he has nothing to do with this."

"I guess he doesn't."

"But Simon." he tried a sad and wistful look, but I wasn't buying it. There was something off, something rehearsed about this performance.

"You were friends, right?"

"We were more than friends."

He was lying; I knew it in my gut but did not know why. "Go on."

"We had been friends for a long time, and the nature of our friendship took on a more intimate nature, and the rules of my marriage forbade an ongoing relationship, so the evening we had the coffee, I had to inform him of this. Which is why he went storming off."

There was a clack of heels as the lady of the house stormed in and slapped him. Both hands went up; this was a stage slap. A theatrical event was obviously being staged for my benefit; why?

"Thank you, detective. Now I know the truth.

"There's still a murder."

"The police will handle that, and since you did your job so quickly, I would like to offer a bonus." She pulled a check for a grand out of her purse, already made out to me. It would have been more realistic if she had taken the time to write the check, but she wanted me out of there quickly. I took the money.

Heading over to the Whitney Bank, I handed it to Fallwell, my new buddy. His eyes got big when he saw the zeros.

"Hey, Fallwell. Do you have a stock division?"

"We have someone who liaisons with New York for our private banking clients such as yourself."

"Great, find out the current share price of BMW."

He went off to another desk, a phone call was made, and he returned. The price is low at .59 a share, but this is not an investment I would advise."

"I will take 1,000 shares. I am confident that this will be worth a million bucks someday".

"It will be against my advice," he cautioned me. "You know their part in the war."

"Do it anyway. I got a hunch."

"Have you finished your business with the La Branche family?"

"It's on hold for the moment."

"If you can spare the time," he grabbed a pen and started writing. "I have a friend who is an insurance agent. He has a suspected case of fraud."

I took the paper, "Thanks for the lead."

I drove over to the address I had been given. It was in the garden district. I found Mr. Foley in his office. It was plush and well-furnished; I suspected they did not pay out many claims.

After the introductions: "Have you got a camera?"

I didn't. "A camera is no problem; tell me what you need?"

"Barry Sommers was a worker at the sausage factory when an equipment malfunction occurred. There is no question he was hurt, but he is claiming long-term disability, and before we pay a big claim, we need to verify if he is indeed disabled. I want you to follow him all day for at least three days, and if you see any evidence of him walking without assistance, take pictures. I will pay you three days upfront."

"You know my rate?"

"Everyone knows your rate, more than twice that of any other Detective, so I expect you are either the best or the most arrogant son of a bitch who ever lived."

"If I am honest, I am a little bit of both."

He cracked a smile. "Good."

I will start first thing in the morning.

The car was coming in handy. I returned to the bank, deposited the check and went camera shopping. I got a good sales guy who showed me how to use it and load film. The film could not be exposed to light, so he had me practice in this little bag until I got it right.

I had a cold supper of carrots, celery, fruit and nuts. I was not going to get fat.

The next morning, dressed and showered, I began my surveillance. I parked a block away from the house and went for a stroll, checking all the angles. I saw the subject come out of the house with apparent difficulty. A female was helping him. He used sticks for walking, and his body was slightly twisted. He was helped into an auto, and off they went. I took the opportunity to explore the house.

It was a nice place for Chalmette; I looked in all the windows, modest but tastefully furnished. It even had a pool out back and sunchairs. There was a high fence, but there were gaps large enough to get a sense of the yard.

The weather was changeable this time of year, but there were days when the pool could be put to use. We could be 50 one day and 75 the next. Rain would appear out of nowhere and pummel the city for 5 minutes or 5 hours.

I could see the front of the house from the car; I waited til dark, peeing in bushes and drinking from a canteen. I was hungry when I got home and went out for a proper dinner. That meant my catfish po boy was served on a china plate, not paper.

I got up early, went swimming and then drove back to the house. The Sommers still had yet to return, so I parked in the same place. If they noticed the car, they would think it was a neighbour. They returned just before dusk, and he moved just slightly faster. Maybe they had visited a physical therapist.

I drove to the one Chinese joint out in Metairie and got beef and broccoli. The sauce was a little too thick for my taste, but it was nice to have broccoli. The beef was tastier than I remembered beef being, and I had to sort my brain and realise I was remembering the future. I was going to have to hit a steakhouse. Meat in this era was a prize.

The next day, the heat came back. I wanted to wear a Hawaiian shirt, but that was too loud, so I settled for a white shirt with sleeves rolled. No one went in or out of the house, so I took a little walk. I peered into the back gate, and both of the Sommers were lying on sun chairs naked as the day they were born. Then Mr. got up, strolled into the kitchen and got a beer.

I got in the car and drove to the alley behind the house. I climbed onto the hood so I had a view over the fence and got a few shots waiting for him to spot me. As soon as he did, he screamed at me. "Pervert", and got up running towards me. Just as the gate opened, I started the car and drove away. I took the film to the development centre and was told I had to wait a day. I let him know there were unclothed people on the roll, but it was not obscene and then slipped him a five-spot to be discreet.

It was only 5 p.m., so I dropped by the Health Club to see if Michael was free for dinner. Not only was he free, but he knew a place. We left our cars in the lot and walked over to Galitore's.

I had my first oysters. Even in the year 2,000, the American North was not oyster country. Minnesota had lake fish and frozen Tilapia. We had sablefish stuffed with crawfish drenched in a brandy cream sauce. I asked for vegetables, so a side of creamed spinach was served. We split a bottle of wine, and surprisingly, he chose an American Chardonnay. "This one has no oak. It is aged in stainless and very fruit forward with enough acid to cut the sauce's richness."

We strolled back to the club in the warm evening, and I took my car home.

After a good night's sleep, I picked up my photos and drove to the insurance company.

"Fraud, as you suspected." He laughed when he saw the pictures and gave me a bonus. I liked this job. People just handed me money. I took the money and appreciated the irony. This was the same insurance company that I had scammed.

To the bank, I went.

I still had an unsolved murder. When I get too far in my head, I put it back in my body. I went to the club and lifted hard and heavy. There was only one guy in the sauna when I entered. I gave him a nod and lay down in one of the wooden chairs. After a few minutes. "Excuse me, sir."

I opened one eye. "What?"

He held out his hand. "Ensign Jacob Jordan, sir, I served under Lieutenant Potts, Mr. Evans. I hear you are the one investigating his murder."

I wanted to meet a man wearing pants one day, but I sat up. He had my attention. He was young, baby-faced and clean-shaven above the neck.

"What can you tell me about Potts?"

"There are rumours, sir, because of the place he came out of before he was shot, but those rumours are not true. I joined up just when I was 18. I was serving when his wife was killed, and I saw what grief did to him. Since the war ended, the ships have been in maintenance and training mode. I have not seen active duty, but I know why he wanted to join recruiting and stay in New Orleans. He had a girl out in Slidell. I met her three days before he died. I was out with some of the guys, and they came out of a shop on Royal. She was clearly with child, sir. I think Lieutenant Potts may be the father. We had been here six months before; she was about that far along. He wanted a family more than anything, Sir."

"Have you told anyone else this?"

"I have no one to tell."

"Did you come here just to find me?"

"That was a happy accident; the club gives each of us a packet of day passes when we are in port, their way of supporting the troops. I was going to head over to your office after my swim, but here you are, sir."

"Do you know where this girl lives or her name?"

"Her name is Janelle, Sir, but Slidell is a small town. Just drive over the bridge until you smell the sulphur and start asking for Janelle."

"Do you remember what she looks like?'

"She was very petite, bordering on tiny, no more than 4 feet 10 inches. She had dark hair and a pretty face but a short haircut—not like a man but short for a woman. Her hair was combed but not styled. She may not even know what happened if she didn't read the papers."

"Thanks, Jacob. I will find her."

Halfway across the bridge, I started to smell the sulfur. After the first exit off the bridge, there was a trailer park. I stopped in the rental office. A bleach blond sidled up to the desk like every step was an invitation. "How can I help you?" I would have told her, but there wasn't time.

"I only have a first name. I am looking for a girl named Janelle, who is about six months pregnant."

"Good news or bad?"

"Bad, very bad."

"She has a trailer over on lot 11, and I'll go get her and bring her here. Someone has to pick up the pieces when you leave."

Janelle came in barefoot, her feet too swollen for shoes. She was very pretty and much more far along than six months.

"Hey Janelle, I'm John; when are you due?"

She put her hand on her midsection. "Any minute if you want to know the truth. Baby's father is supposed to be here, but sometimes, he has to stay on the ship. I hope he gets here before I pop."

"That your husband?"

She nodded. "His name is Simon. We got married six months ago when I told him about the baby. As soon as he is relieved from active duty, we are going to find a little house."

I secretly hoped she had read the papers, but the girl didn't know the man she was counting on was dead. I was going to have to tell her. This part was always so easy in movies, TV shows and books. The detective would use his compassionate voice to deliver the news; after a single tear, they would cut to the commercial, the next scene, or the next chapter.

I was about to cry myself. "Look, I got no easy way to say this, but you haven't seen Simon because Simon was murdered.

She screamed and began to sob. She fell against the blonde, who held her like a baby. I was not going to try and question her now. I left my card on the counter and murmured the useless phrase about being sorry for her loss. And then her water broke. The blonde and I helped her to my car, and we raced off to the hospital.

Once she was in the delivery room, the blonde turned to me. "Hello, John, I'm Kim."

"Hello, Kim. I am pleased to meet you even if the circumstances are not ideal."

We waited, but not very long.

The baby came quickly. Kim said she wanted to stay with the mother and would find a ride home.

I made my way back, sickened at how relieved I was to be away from this.

Chapter 12

Back in the office, I sat and contemplated when a lady came in. She was in her 60s, but in the way only women with money can be. Dyed hair, perfect makeup, perfect nails, perfect clothes, clearly made for her body. This was not an off-the-rack kind of woman.

"I am the original Mrs La Branche, Brian's mother. You have been investigating, and you were at the house today. I want you to tell me everything you know."

"Ask your son; you are not my client; loose lips get guys like me shot."

She sighed and rolled her eyes, pulling her chequebook out of a small clutch bag.

"How much will it take to loosen your lips?"

"Like I already told you, you are not my client."

"Did you solve the murder?"

"If I did, it would be in the papers."

"Why are you so obstinate?"

"Why are you so arrogant?"

We were at a standstill; she stood there like a statue, but her brain was working. I could almost see the gears spinning.

"Can I hire you?"

"What's the case?"

"I want you to solve the murder of this military man and communicate to me any ancillary information you pick up."

"I don't trade in gossip."

"How many days will it take to solve this case?"

"I don't know. When I have a lead, I follow it."

"Have you any leads?"

"One."

"Why did my daughter-in-law dismiss you?"

"She didn't. She got what she wanted."

"So she did not hire you to solve this murder and attempted murder of my son?"

"What she hired me for is confidential, but she got what she wanted and no longer needs my services."

She sat down, got out her chequebook and wrote me a check for $500. "Stay with it, find the shooter, follow every lead. There is more where that came from. What's your telephone number?"

"I haven't got a phone; give me your number, and if I learn something, I will drop a dime."

"What kind of detective are you?"

"What kind of woman are you?"

She tried to look offended, but I could see the smile. If she were 30 years younger, I suspect she would have shown me what kind of woman she was.

I went to a bar, not the type of bar where you drink good wine or the kind that stinks of piss and beer, but the kind where you have a whiskey and maybe a conversation.

I sat alone at the end of the bar when I noticed a lady who had dressed to be noticed. She wanted to be seen, and I enjoyed the view. Eventually, I sauntered over. "Would you like some company tonight?"

"Feel free to join me, sir."

We exchanged the usual pleasantries, and we were both fine and had nice days. I found out she was divorced and had two kids. She lived out of town but had come to New Orleans to look for a job. She wanted to make a move. The kids were with her sister, so she was as free as a bird. Eventually, I got around to offering a nightcap at my place. She accepted.

"Whisky or wine?" that was all I had to offer. When I brought out the whiskey, it began to rain, one of those rains that felt like it was scouring the city. When her glass was empty, she declined more.

"Are you sure you want to go out in this storm?"

"What are you suggesting, sir," faux outrage.

"I was going to suggest an umbrella, but clearly, you have something else in mind."

"I don't know what you are talking about."

"Yes, you do. You see, women and men are not all that different. We want the same things. It's just that women are trained from girlhood on to pretend they are a rare breed with no desire. I don't believe it, do you?"

She slapped me, and then she kissed me. It was the kind of kiss that told me she was not going anywhere, at least not until the morning.

I did things with her she told me no man had ever done before. She was a screamer, but the neighbours thought the house was haunted, so if they heard her over the rain, it wouldn't matter. It has been so long that I felt electricity course through my body from my toes to the back of my head. I may have screamed myself. Once was not enough, so neither of us got much sleep.

She declined coffee. I had no milk.

"It's time for the walk of shame."

"Try it another way, hold your head high, be proud and never be ashamed again."

She kissed me on the cheek and went out the door.

It was only then I realised, I never got her name. Also, I didn't own an umbrella.

I guess it didn't matter.

I figured I should leave the new mother alone for a few days, but maybe I could help her. I returned to the port—this time, I gave my name and was given immediate access. Commander Martin took me back to his headquarters.

"What did you learn?"

"I learned I am being conned. Mr La Branche could not wait to tell me he and Simon were lovers so that his wife, on cue, could give him a slap and me a bonus for solving nothing. I learned that Potts got married six months ago after getting a girl pregnant, and that was his reason for wanting to leave active service and get into recruiting. The shock made the baby pop in record time when I told his wife what happened. I learned that the senior Mrs La Branche thinks something funny is going on, so she gave a huge advance to keep on the case and report to her. I hope to learn that the Navy has some way of caring for the new widow with a new baby."

"You work fast."

"So I'm told."

"There will be a 10k payout to Simon's next of kin, which would be?"

"Janelle, if she took his name, Janelle Potts."

"Simon enlisted in our ranks in 1922, so the pension is also hers and not insubstantial after more than 20 years."

"She has a baby now; how long will this take?"

"I can expedite the insurance; it's our own fund, not an outside agency. There will be a lot of paperwork for the pension, but I can help her with it. It could take about 3 to 6 months."

"The insurance should be enough scratch to keep her in diapers. They just bought a house, and when I talk to her, I will find out what she needs to collect the pension."

"The house is paid for. Simon kept the news of his new wife quiet, but he paid cash for the house. It's a little townhouse out in Metairie, one of those new developments where six houses ring a shared swimming pool."

"I'll see if I can scare up a lawyer at the Health club to help her with the paperwork on the house."

"Do you know someone?"

"No, I'll just get my dingaling out in the sauna and use it for bait."

He gave me a puzzled look.

"I meet everyone in the sauna; it's like a naked old boys club. Maybe I will try the bar; I would like to meet someone while wearing pants."

"He laughed. Now I know what you mean. They give us day passes when we are in port. You think of the sauna as a place to relax, but they use it to do business. I hear the mob does this as well; no chance of wearing a wire."

We both laughed.

After leaving, I drove to Slidell to see if I could find Kim. She was in the office, but her walk and demeanour were different today; tragedy can do that.

"Today, I come with good news. Is the mother out of the hospital yet?"

"They are keeping her one more day. Then I guess she will come back here."

"She can move when she's ready. Simon paid cash for the house, so with the help of a lawyer, it will be her place free and clear. She will also get the life insurance in a few days and his pension once the paperwork has cleared."

"I am so relieved. She was a waitress until she got too far along, but it is hard to work when you are a new mother. I will let her know today."

"No pressure, but I still have a murder to solve, and at some point, I am going to ask her to talk about Simon. When she's ready, as long as she's ready soon."

"That reminds me, you forgot to put your number on your card."

"I got no phone. Like everything else, Ma Bell works slow around here."

"I got that. You swing around in a couple of days, and I will see if our girl is up to talking. Babies don't stop grief, but they do distract."

I sat in my office for a few hours, made notes and got nowhere. At 5:30, I decided to hit the bar at my club and see who I could scare up.

I parked, signed in, and went down the hall to the bar. I went in and took a stool. I saw a lot of mixed drinks; I don't like juice ruining the flavour of my booze. "Bourbon, neat."

"Yes, sir." The bartender was a lady, tall and dark, with a face that said both welcome and don't fuck with me, at the same time. She put it down in front of me.

"Enjoy Detective." She was letting me know she knew who I was.

"You seem to know everyone, even those you have never met. Have we got a lawyer in this crowd?"

"Three, what kind of law?"

"Estate, with real estate involved, someone who might help out a lady in need, pro bono.

"Jesse Duplantis, family money, good practice, soft heart. He's the redhead playing darts.

I took a stool nearby. "Mr Duplantis, I'd like a minute when you finish your game." He won the game and walked over.

"Detective Evans, we have never met; how do you know who I am?"

"How do you know who I am?"

"Fair point. What can I do for you?"

"You heard about the murder of Simon Potts?" I could tell from his face he had. "Simon left behind a widow who just had a baby yesterday, and she hasn't got any money, at least not right now. Simon bought a house, paid cash, and now it is hers. We need to get the deed in her name, and she may need some advice on dealing with the taxes. Pro bono, or at least delayed billing til she can collect the life insurance. "

"Did he leave a will?'

"Not that we know of."

"I know a judge over in family court who will be sympathetic. I'll see him; it is a simple matter of amending the deed. I won't charge her." He handed me a card. "Just have her give me a call, and I will be happy to take care of it."

"Thanks."

"So it seems Simon was not as he is rumoured to be."

"No, and unless you know this town well, it's just a coffee spot. I was there myself."

I could see the curious looks, so I got out of there before I became the subject of an investigation.

Chapter 13

It took me a while to invite the sandman in, I kept thinking about what my next step should be.

I hadn't taken a break since I arrived, so I decided to take two days off, like a weekend. I had been going nonstop since I got here, and pretending to be a detective was taking a toll on me. Like a pit bull, I believed in taking hold and not letting go until something shook loose.

Since the night had been rocky, I stayed in bed and drifted back off. Mid-morning when I hit the club, was a really quiet time. I had the pool to myself and swam like my life depended on it. I decided to stay out of the sauna today. I didn't want to go through the third degree.

I went down and noticed the barber opposite the bar was open. I went in and got myself cleaned up.

Afterwards, I popped into Michael's office, and he invited me to lunch. He knew a place I HAD to try. Why not? I had jumped on the scale and all of my fat was psychological. I had not gained an ounce.

We took his car and drove over to Uglesich's, it looked like nothing from the outside but the food was like nothing I had ever tasted. I had a mixed plate of BBQ shrimp and oysters. It was nothing like the vile, sweet red sauce people glop on food and call BBQ; this was a buttery, garlic, savoury mouth bomb. Micheal had shrimp and sausage cakes topped with a creole cream sauce and we shared the butter-fried potatoes. They qualified as a vegetable.

We discussed the case and how I had learned a lot, and everything I learned put another layer of mud on the mess.

He asked about the location of Brian's injury. I told him it was in the calf just below the knee, but I could not be sure how serious it was because he had so much protective padding.

"That will be hard on him. He likes to spend time on his knees and is not a man who prays."

I liked that he trusted me enough to be catty and queeny with me. "What else can you tell me about him?"

"Little Miss Brian likes to befriend straight men, invite them to the house to meet the wife, go on hikes, even camping and fishing, and then make a play. Some are flattered or complimented. Others walk away, and once he was punched in the eye. He likes trade."

"So it sounds like his friendship with Potts was part of a pattern?"

"Yes, and because he has made the rounds with so many in New Orleans, he needs sailors and occasional visitors unaware of his reputation."

Did I say day off … .? I lied.

The next day, I hit the weights early. I asked for three towels when I signed in. I liked the sauna, but thus far, it had been a social hub, not a relaxing place to be.

After my workout, I rinsed off. The extensive sauna room was empty, so I laid one towel on the wooden-style deck chair. Once I got on top of it, I put the other towel from my face down. My legs below the knees were visible, but I had effectively blocked out the world.

After about 5 minutes, I heard two voices. I tuned out, trying to stay in my meditative state. And then I heard it, "That detective." I tuned in, and at first, it was just gossip about how fast I moved when I came to town and the faux outrage that I would buy a house so quickly. "First place he even saw, now who does that? You get an agent and take your time. That's your home."

"He's got no wife, no kids and is friendly with the coffee house crowd."

"No, Miss Boudreaux, who lives across the street from him, saw a woman coming out in the morning. And no matter who they are or their status, he treats everybody the same. Even black folks."

"We do, too, at least those who have money." Gleeful laughter.

"That's the strange thing. The good old boys who run this town seem to have accepted him."

"It makes sense all of them may need his services. They all have complicated lives."

"Lunch shift is going to begin soon. We had better get over to the cafe."

When they left, I lowered my towel. I waited, giving them time to move on before I left. I felt like I was melting when I got to the shower. I got dressed and went downstairs.

Elsie was at the sign-in desk. "Elsie, those two men who left a few minutes ago, what cafe do they work at?"

"You mean Martin and Ben? They are thick as thieves. They are both servers over at Galatoire's.

"Forgive me, we did the introductions so quickly; which one was Martin again?"

"The redhead. I think they are so cute. We don't have many service staff at this club, but they are both determined to move up in the world and are not wrong to make the investment. Some of the men here can be helpful.

"Yeah, it's a great crowd, and they are keeping me busy. "

I walked over to Galatoire's to properly meet my new friends.

They had just finished setting the dining room for lunch service, and there was one lone woman sitting by the window with a glass of wine. I walked over to the redhead. "You must be Martin. Is your buddy Ben around? I'd like to talk with you both."

His face went bright red. "I'll get him, sir."

Ben, equally red, came out from the service station. "It's not busy yet, guys. Can we step outside for a minute?"

We stood on Bourbon Street, and both looked at the sidewalk. I let the silence stand. Finally, Martin spoke. "Was that you under the towel, sir? We were just talking, and we didn't mean anything."

"Talking is what I want you to do. Elsie tells me you are both ambitious; you help me, and I help you. Working in a joint like this, you hear everything about everyone. In my case, I want to know conversations, gossip, or whatever you learn relevant to any of the players. And you will be paid for the info. I want you on my team."

Martin piped up. "Mr and Mrs La Branche were here for dinner two nights ago. They were celebrating something, went all out, even got a bottle of Dom."

"Was the Mr. on crutches?"

Then Ben said, "He was in a suit walked a little stiff, but he said it was only a flesh wound."

"Did either of you overhear any of the conversation?"

Martin looked down, "It was so busy that night, but they are regulars. Next time they come, I will station myself nearby."

"Thanks, men," I gave them each a five spot. "If you hear or see anything else, you know where to find me."

This was getting curiouser and curiouser. I was paid for what exactly? Snooping around, not solving a case, and witnessing a bit of theatre. Why?

I was sitting at my desk when Seargent O'Riley NOPD came in. He flashed his badge and took a seat.

"You are stirring up a ton of manure, son." He was thick but not fat and probably around 40, but he had lived hard, and it showed on his face.

"You got a question?"

"Yeah, I hear you witnessed Mr La Branche making a confession that he was involved with Potts and ending the liaison when a random shooter showed up out of nowhere to shoot his now ex-lover point blank in the chest."

"I got no problem with what any man does with his johnson, but don't the cops go after guys like him?"

"Not the ones with money; we hassle the steam room players and the toilet cruisers from time to time, but those uptown boys are off limits. New Orleans allows all kinds. We just keep an eye on the public spaces so Vice can feel like they are doing something."

"Good to know."

"So you can verify his confession. He and Potts were involved?"

"Why does it matter unless La Branche killed Potts? Why all this interest in who did what to whom?"

"The La Branche family are convinced that Potts had a lover from the ship, who got word of where he was and came and shot him. They believe Potts was going landside to be with La Branche, and the jealous lover shot him."

"Who on the ship have you talked to?"

"Just the commander, seems the boys were out, going from bar to bar, and none of them has an alibi."

"While I did witness the confession, I think it was staged for my benefit. You see, I did a little digging, and Pott got married six months ago and planned on setting up housekeeping out in Metairie with a female who has just given birth to his son."

"Jesus Christ, how'd you find that out?"

"Just doing my job."

"If Potts had been a member of a good family, I would have unlimited money and staff to go after the killer, but as it is, they are pressuring me to close the case and move on."

"Move on if they force you, but don't close the case. I have a new client who is paying me to press on, and I took the lady's money, so I have no choice. Why are you really here? I don't think it's to trade tales about an open investigation."

"Did someone shoot out your front window when you started nosing into this case?"

"Probably kids, rocks, mischief."

He pointed to the right, high up in the wall. "Then what's that bullet doing in your wall?"

"So that's where it went."

"I don't know many men who get shot at who don't call the police."

"I don't have a phone."

"Stop with the smart aleck responses."

"I am new in town, and I don't know the cops here. Some don't like guys like me very much, and I did not want to bring attention to myself."

"That's fair, so who do you think shot at you?"

"The same person who shot Potts. I think it was a warning, but since I am not close to the truth, I can't figure out what they were afraid of.."

"Where do you keep your gun?"

"I don't have a gun."

"You got no telephone, you got no gun, what kind of private Dick are you?"

"The kind that is going to solve this case," I said with more confidence than I felt.

Chapter 14

That night, I dreamed about my old life and woke up with a new resolve. I may have been a fraud, but I was going to fake it 'til I made it and solved this case. I made a strong pot of black coffee. I heard a knock on my door. I went to the front, and it was Commander Martin. "Come in. Can I offer you a cup of coffee? I got no milk and no sugar."

"Black is fine."

I returned with the coffee, and we both sat down. He pulled an envelope out of his pocket.

"I got the insurance settlement for Janelle. Can you drop it off for me?"

"Sure, I was going to check in today."

"I wrote her a note and gave her the contact information for me so I can help her with the pension paperwork when she is ready."

"Whether she is ready to talk or not, I am sure this will take the heat off her."

"And when she feels like it, the boys on the ship would like to meet her and the baby. Potts being shot hit them hard and...."

"I get it, and I will let her know she's got a ship that cares. It never hurts to feel people, even people you have never met, are on your side."

Neither of us was good at small talk, so we finished our coffee, and I drove out to Slydell.

I went to the office. "Good morning, Kim. How is our mother doing today?"

"She is out of the hospital and focused on the baby. It's a boy, she named him Simon."

"I got a check for her, Simon's life insurance. As the widow, she is entitled to it." I handed Kim the check.

"I will take it over to her. This will help."

"And when she's ready to hear it, I got more good news."

Kim, envelope in her hand. "I'll be right back."

When she returned, she had Janelle with her and was holding a very tiny baby. She looked at me clear-eyed and determined. "I am ready to talk to you, detective."

"I am going to skip the sorrys and congratulations because neither will mean a damn thing. I'll get right to the point. Simon bought a townhouse in Metairie and paid cash, and it's your place free and clear. Here is the business card of Jesse Duplantis, a lawyer I know. He will help you with the deed and any other issues with the estate.

"Mr......"

"There's more. Commander Martin will work with you to ensure you get Simon's pension as the widow. You won't have to return to work so that you can raise this kid right."

A single tear rolled down her face: relief, sadness, or maybe both.

"Are you up to taking some questions?"

"I can handle it."

She was tiny but strong. "So, start at the beginning, tell me how you met when you married, give me the whole story. I got nothing but time.'

"My parents died in a car crash when I was 19. I was a few months into Dental hygienist school when I had to drop out.

I got work over at Bayou Bar. It's a nice place, with good food and good tips.

Neighbourhood. Friendly. I have been there seven years, and the owners are good to me. I pick the nights I want to work. Maybe it was fate, but I was not on the schedule the night I met Simon. They called the office and asked Kim to send me in. It was a Monday, and Hope, the Monday girl, called in sick. It was just me and the bartender with a smattering of customers. Simon came in alone. He said he was hungry, and I could tell he was lonely. Since the night was slow, I brought him his burger, and we talked. Men may not be much for talking, but when they get a sympathetic ear, that changes."

"What did you talk about?"

"The death of his pregnant wife. They had given up on kids, and then when she was finally with child, she was killed. And I told him about my parents. Does your car have a lap belt?"

"Yeah."

"Use it. They should add a second belt that straps your chest back so your head can't rock forward. Too many people die in these crashes."

"Someday they will."

"So we both had experienced a loss, and we just connected. We closed the bar at 9, business was slow, and we walked down by the river. He was a gentleman, not like most guys; he walked me to my car and asked if we could meet again.

"How often did you meet?"

"I don't know if you know, but New Orleans is home base for those three ships at the port. Since the war ended, they just went on training missions and returned for maintenance. It is all about readiness right now, not real active duty. So we got to see each other often. We went down the romance path pretty quick, and soon, I was pregnant. He almost jumped for joy when I told him, and we married right away before I started to show. He must have wanted to surprise me with the house. He was a good guy, through and through."

"Have you got any idea why anyone on earth would want him dead?"

A second tear rolled down her face. She wiped it away. "None. I met one of the men from his ship a short time ago. Sweet kid, baby face. But we mostly kept to ourselves and made plans for his job change."

"When was that going to go into effect?"

"January 1. Now I have to stay strong and focus on Simon Junior."

"By the way, you have an entire ship of men who want to meet you and the baby. He will have no shortage of Uncles when you are ready."

She stood up; I could see she was barely holding her emotions in check. "Not yet, but soon. Thanks for coming by, but I think we need a little rest now."

I blew her a kiss as she walked away. She was all fine china on the outside and all forged steel inside. I had great respect for her.

I sat in my car. I kept thinking this should all be obvious somehow. Maybe my brain was damaged when I made the time transition, but I was at the end of my ideas. I decided to check in with my boys Martin and Ben and see if they had overheard anything worthwhile.

Lunch was just starting to percolate when I arrived, so they came to me one at a time. "No sir, we have nothing now."

Feeling defeated, I walked to the French Market. No matter how this case turned out, I needed to eat.

Not a lot available. Carrots, apples, cabbage. While staring at the cabbage, I heard a voice behind me.

"You thinking about making a coleslaw, Mr. Evans?"

I turned around; it was Syliva, the La Branche housekeeper. "To tell the truth, I am not much of a cook. I don't know how to make coleslaw."

"Shred some cabbage, carrots and apples if you like; add mayonnaise, a little sugar and just a touch of vinegar."

"I hate sugar."

"Then don't put any sugar in it. Problem solved. How have you been surviving?"

"Bacon, eggs, fruit and nuts and fried catfish po boys."

"The bachelor's dilemma. Someday, someone will open a cooking school for bachelors and make a fortune. Can you turn on the oven and boil water?"

"That much I can do."

"Then, get some fish and butter, salt, pepper, and some sliced cabbage and carrots in a pan. Turn your oven to 350. Bring a cup of water to a boil, add ½ cup rice, put a lid on the rice, turn the heat low and put the fish in the oven. Check your watch; 20 minutes later, it will all be done perfectly."

"That reminds me, I still have to get a watch."

She laughed heartily. "There is no fixing men; men gonna do the way men gonna do, no matter how much we try and help."

"I am going to prove you wrong. I am buying rice and fish and getting a watch today."

"I have to get running, but when I see you next, you let me know how that fish was."

"I certainly will."

"Goodbye, Mr. Evans."

"Goodbye, Miss Sylvia."

I bought rice, fish, butter, cabbage, apples and a pan with a lid to cook the rice in. Then I bought a watch on the way home. Damn, if she wasn't right, this was the best meal I had ever cooked and not hard at all. I even opened some wine. I ate at my desk because I still had no dining table, but it felt good.

Chapter 15

I woke very early, went for a swim and ran into no one I knew. I could tell from some of the looks that they knew me, but no one approached, and I was not in the mood to talk.

At 9:30 a.m., I hit the phone booth on the corner. "Mrs. La Branche, please, John Evans here."

"One moment, sir." I heard her voice over the covered phone. "Are you in for Mr. Evans?

"Of course I am.

"I am calling to offer you your money back. I am getting nowhere. I resolved things for Potts Widow, but you did not hire me to do social work."

"I want you to stay with it. I want my son's reputation unblemished, and until this is resolved, people will continue to think he had something to do with it." She could count on me in that group; I just couldn't figure out what or why.

"Try this; I saw it in a movie once. A detective with no leads put out the word that the witnesses had finally made an identification. It could frighten out the murderer from their little cave."

"You're the boss."

I did not spread the rumour; I wasn't comfortable working that way. But if the lady wanted me to keep her money and press on. I would do it.

I made another phone call to the junior La Branche residence. "Good morning, La Branche residence."

"Good morning Sylvia, John Evans."

Her voice warmed. "I am sorry, Mr. Evans, but the house is empty this morning. Mr. La Branche had his first day back at the office and the Mrs. is shopping. Seems like she buys a new outfit every other day."

"Good, I wanted to talk to you. You were absolutely right. The fish and the rice were perfect. Any chance you would be willing to give me some cooking lessons?"

"As much as I would enjoy it, it would be a scandal waiting to happen. You can't come here, and if I were to show up at your house and spend time alone with you, I would be hung from a tree before I could get home and tuck my son in. But if you see me at the market, you can ask me anything, and I will share some tips."

"Would it still be a scandal if your husband came over and we made it a dinner party? You work with me in the kitchen, your husband watches over us, and we all eat together."

"Are you colour blind? White men don't be asking black folks to dinner parties in New Orleans. And even if I were white, you make as much a day as I make in a month."

"I'm from Chicago; I don't know the rules."

"I have got to visit this Chicago one day; I'll be in touch." She was laughing as she put down the phone.

I went to the club and lifted. For me, it was meditation time and stress relief. I hit the sauna, and who should I spy but Jesse Duplantis? The carpet matched the drapes. He approached me.

"I am glad you grabbed me; it was pretty easy to sort out the deed as Potts had already put Janelle's name on it. Janelle is moving this weekend, and her friend Kim said there is not much in the way of furniture to move, and she will load her trunk and take care of it. I deal with a lot of grief and families fighting over money, and it was nice to meet a mother so focused on the happiness of her little boy. She is one strong woman."

"You don't know the half of it, but I agree."

"So, are you getting anywhere on the murder thing?"

"No."

"Would you have a few days to track down a lost heir? It's boring work. Mrs Bates left a small fortune to her grandson, and according to her, he moved 'to the city,' but we have no idea which city. You would be checking phone directories, maybe newspapers, until you find the kid. Then, you would have to verify his identity. Once you finish, submit a bill for the number of days it takes, and you can come over to my office on North Rampart and use the phone once you have some leads. I will front your payment and expenses until the estate is settled."

"How much is the estate?"

"Close to one million US dollars if you add in the real estate value."

"You know I have no phone, so you must also know my daily rate."

"I know this town pretty well; it thrives on gossip. You might even start there. The young man's first name was Anthony. He moved away three years ago at the age of 18, presumably to attend a University. Grandma wrote him one check before he left, and he cleared it here. No further support was sent. We have been looking through her correspondence, but young men are not the best at keeping up with letters. She was a hoarder, and we can't possibly go through it all, but if you want to check there, feel free."

"I'll start tonight; what about his parents? Are they still alive?"

"They sure are; they have a place over on Constance Street. When I asked about their son, they said they were estranged, and when I asked Mr. Bates about his mother, I got the same response. They have no interest in contesting the will; they have their own money.

The next morning, I drove up to the Bates' house on Constance Street, and Mrs Bates answered the door. 'Yes, can I help you?"

I gave her my whole rap and then said I was looking for her son, and the ice turned to stone.

"We are estranged."

"He is your only son; what could he have done?'

"It is more than what he has done; it is his very nature. I bid you good day." She shut the door. I have never in my life had someone wish me a good day that sounded more like fuck you."

As I drove away, I had an idea: the penny had finally dropped. I went to the antique shop to see Ettiene and Nigel. I was given the royal greeting and offered tea. I took a cup, black. They doctored their own with milk and sugar.

"Thanks for the hospitality. Did either of you know Anthony Bates?" Nigel blushed a deep red, and my suspicions were confirmed. "So Nigel, where did he go?"

"I don't know, and that's the truth. He left without a word to anyone. You know his parents threw him out of the house when he was 16 when they caught him with a boy?"

"I didn't know. Where did he go?"

"He lived with his grandmother until he was old enough to go out on his own. There were rumours he enlisted, but that is very unlikely. He was the type of boy who could not hide his nature."

"Effeminate?"

"Not in a loud or overt way, but it was such a part of him that he was unable to hide it."

"Where do you think he might have gone?"

"New York or San Francisco. Call Berkeley. They are known for being a haven for students of his type."

"While here, can you two help me with a dining table? I want one that seats six, nothing fancy, simple and plain American woodworking."

Ettiene got excited. "The simplest I have is a 1780 French Beech with eight matching chairs. The woodwork is exquisite but solid and simple, and I know a seamstress who would happily whip up some chair cushions."

"How much would this treasure set me back?"

"Two hundred dollars, and I will throw in the cushions for free."

"Deliver it this week, and you have a deal."

I wrote the check. When they told me how pleased they were to have me as a customer, I could see how true that was.

I went to Jesse's office and called U.C. Berkeley. I had this wrapped up in one day. The kid was in class; they brought him to the phone. I gave him the news about his grandmother, and the tears were real, I had no doubt. I told him about the money and suggested a trip home to confirm his identity and deal with the lawyer. Real estate needs signatures.

Jesse happily wrote me a check for the fee. If I had indeed known the value of a buck in 1945, I would have set a much lower rate. My ignorance was paying off.

Chapter 16

Just as evening began to set, I got a knock on my door. "Door's open."

In came a very large black man.

"Good evening, sir; they call me Big John."

"They call me Evans; you must be Sylvia's husband."

"Yes sir, I am, and I come about you inviting us over for supper."

"I don't have many friends in this town. I hope you will come."

"In New Orleans, sir, white men and black men don't generally sit down at the same table."

"You may not believe me, but segregation is due to end, and I believe in giving things a head start."

"I would not want to be the man who ruined your reputation, sir."

"There is nothing I value more than having a bad reputation; I live in a haunted house, I am a Yankee, and my reputation is already soiled."

"Well then, we would be grateful for the hospitality. What night do you want us here?"

"Does Friday work? I have the feeling you go to church on Sunday and would not want to be out too late on Saturday night."

"You know that's right, Sylvia wants our boy raised in the church. My Mama can watch our son on Friday; what time do you want us here?"

"Sylvia is going to help me prepare this feast, so how about 6:30? Then we can eat by 8:00 if all goes well."

"We will be here. You have a good evening." And with that, he left. A bad reputation was something I could look forward to.

A few minutes later, the bell rang again. It was Ettiene and Giles with my table. I helped carry it into the third room. Once it was in place, they looked around. Giles was appalled at my makeshift closet. "Where is your chifferobe?"

"There is a lot of stuff I have to get around to.

"Do you even have dishes?"

"I gotta get some of them too before I have guests for dinner this weekend."

Giles took a deep breath. "Do you trust us?"

"Sure, I do."

"We pick up a lot of estates in order to get the valuable items. This means we have a lot of furniture we can't move in the shop. We have China cabinets, chifforobes, dressers, china, silver, curtains etc. We get that you like basic, simple things, so let us finish decorating this house and make it a home. We promise nothing frilly or fancy."

"How much would this cost me?"

"This would be the stuff we dump in used furniture stores, so for $50.00, we can do the whole place. We will run over to the warehouse and start this afternoon."

I gave 'em cash.

True to their word, 4 hours later, I was helping them move the furniture in place. I had china, glasses, and silver (plate, not sterling) for twelve people. My clothes were hung and folded correctly, and I had a comfy leather chair and a reading lamp in my bedroom. I was most impressed with the mirrors. They hung them strategically so that I could see every entrance to the room from anywhere in the room. They also doubled as light reflectors, making each room seem larger.

"I really appreciate your work, gentlemen. Let me take you out for a drink."

"We are not country club discreet; everyone knows that we are together. Are you sure you want to be seen with us in public?"

"Definitely. I am working on ruining my reputation, and today is a great day to start."

We headed over to Famous Door, which was quiet and smelled of stale beer. We took a table at the front. I got a whisky neat, and the gents had Gloria Swanson champagne cocktails. I had forgotten about her, but she was still movie star famous, and Sunset Boulevard was yet to come.

I raised a glass to their decorating skills, and by the second drink, they were just a little giddy.

I asked again what they had witnessed; since we were friends, they might be more forthcoming.

Giles answered. "Any hair was under the big hat, but he had the fine features of a blond. In profile, in the half-light, it looked like your friend from over at NOAC, Michael.

"I was with him that night, so I know that's impossible," I told him.

"I can't shake the feeling that I know him, but nothing comes to me."

"If a name pops into your head, call the police and then send for me. I got a client paying me to know who did this."

"It had to be personal, 'cause Brian was just injured just enough so's he could not run to the cops."

Ettienne spoke. "Can we get away from murder for a minute and talk about how gorgeous your house is now?"

"Yeah, we can. Thanks to you two. I feel at home here. I am no longer a visitor."

A fine-featured, not-too-tall man. That description chewed at my brain.

The next day, I returned to the coffee shop to look at faces. Brian La Branche had worked his way through the locals and was focused on the military. He may have broken a few hearts in the process. Jealousy is often the reason for murder. One of the guys may have assumed he was involved with Potts and wanted to punish him—short, delicate features. I got a cup of coffee and just looked around. I got a lot of looks in response, but no one approached. I spent a good hour watching men come and go, often in pairs. I decided to stake the joint for a couple of days.

I came back to catch the after-work crowd. I was shocked at the number of wedding rings, but shouldn't have been. Considering the time, most men conformed to social norms, and norms did not regulate desire. The dick wants what the dick wants. No law can control humans, especially men.

I looked at all kinds of faces. Petite, refined features were not the norm. New Orleans was a melting pot of French, Italian, Spanish, Irish, and even Hungarian, but most men were dark with strong features.

I decided to come back on the weekend.

Friday morning, I set my alarm to get to NOAC the moment it opened. It had been a few days since my last workout, and I needed the stress release that weights gave me. I saw a few faces I knew and managed to get away with a simple wave. The sauna was empty, a fact for which I was grateful. I love the heat, but it was such a coffee klatch old boys' club. It was nice to have it to myself.

After I showered, I walked over to the French Market. I love a good roast chicken, and today's chicken had so much more going on than the chicken of my time. It was a luxury item, more expensive than beef or pork, but I found a nice one hanging at the Poultry Lady stall. She had one she called the Queen of Chickens, descended from a French Bresse. It was expensive so I bought it.

Then, I picked up everything fresh and healthy I could find, including some mushrooms I had never tried called Morel. Since I was on foot, I stopped at the wine store and picked up two bottles of White Bordeaux and one Cremant, just in case.

Once I had everything put away, I walked, looking at faces and going nowhere. I ended up by the river. I sat on a bench, and it was only when I saw a vendor wagon selling gumbo ya ya I realised that I had yet to eat breakfast or lunch. It was served in a large Dixie paper cup with a wooden spoon and went down easy.

As I walked home, scanning faces as I went and took a short nap before setting the table. Ettiene and Giles did an excellent job picking things out. Elegant but simple. No flowers or funny patterns on anything.

Soon, the time arrived, and Sylvia and Big John knocked on my back door. They had gone around the house so as not to be noticed. I let them in and poured the wine.

Sylvia feigned shock. "We have a meal to prepare; you don't want me drunk."

Big John laughed. "Drunk or sober, you the best cook this city knows."

"Thank you." She took a sip. "This is good, it must be French."

"It is." I got the chicken out. "Teach me how to roast this thing."

"It's got blue feet. Is that a Queen?"

"That's what she called it."

"You got yourself a fine bird. What do you have for sauce?"

She checked my refrigerator and approved most of my selections. "John, run to the market and get some heavy cream for the sauce."

"Yes, Ma'am," I replied.

"Not you, Mr. Evans, my John."

"You are in my house; you don't have to call me Mr Evans. Big John calls me Evans."

"Please understand me; It is not my being formal and standoffish. I run into you in public: I don't want to slip. There are different rules for black and white in this town. There are different rules for men and women, too; if you take your car to my husband and he calls you Evans at the shop, it will be overlooked because he is a man. I call you Evans in public, and everyone who sees us will think you know what I look like under my clothes, and we will both be judged. When I call you Mr. Evans, it is self-protection."

"I don't like it, but I understand."

Big John laughed, "I will get the cream, and when I come back, I want you both fully dressed."

"That man is a caution. Have you got a cleaver?"

"Yes, I do."

"You want to learn, and you learn by doing. I will talk you through this, but I am not lifting a finger to help. Cut off the head and feet, and then you will brown them in butter with chopped shallot."

The next thing I knew, we were foraging in the backyard for wild herbs; I am ashamed to admit I had never been in my own yard. I had a banana tree, a fig tree and a lot of herbs, including the thyme we were looking for. Big John returned with the cream, and when the broth from the feet and head had reduced, we added the mushrooms and cream just as the chicken was finishing his roast in the oven. Following instructions, I had vegetable sides and perfect rice.

Soon, we were sitting down to dinner, and I was shocked at how good it tasted. "I cannot believe I cooked this."

"You can cook; most men can. All I did was tell you a recipe; you can also read one from a book and follow the instructions. All cooking at the beginning is following the instructions, then you can improvise once you get practice.

"What cookbook would you suggest?"

"Lena Richards's cookbook was published about five or so years ago, and she is one of the greats for capturing the local flavours. You live here now, and she will teach you how to cook like it. I got one cookbook I can give you. The government gave it out; it has Wartime recipes and ways to get by when there was rationing. The folks I work for always had the money for the black market, so rationing never applied to them, and black folks always knew how to get by. I did try the biscuit recipe made out of potatoes; it's not a real biscuit but a good bite to eat when the flour gets low."

Big John laughed. "I loved those things; I wish you would make them again."

"Alright then, I will make up a batch before church on Sunday, and you can have them with your coffee." Then, "We don't have a proper breakfast on Sunday, just a bite so everyone is ready for a big dinner after church."

"Can I ask a personal question of both?"

"Why not?"

"Are you descended from slaves?"

"Big John is, we have the bill of sale of his great grandfather, but I am descended from a free woman of colour, mistress of a French man, and she owned slaves."

"That is so fucked up."

This brought laughter from them both; Sylvia held up a finger. "Watch your language, Mr. Evans."

Big John cut in, "He's right, it is fucked up, New Orleans is all fucked up."

"So why do you go to church? You know that is not the religion of your ancestors."

"Sylvia comes from the Voodoo tradition."

"You hush."

"You know it's true, and you still do some of those rituals, and me, I don't even know what the religion from Africa was, and I figure one is as good as another. Religion doesn't care if you believe; you just nod and smile, gossip a little at the potlucks and find a way to fit in."

We had gone through both bottles of wine, and I opened the bubbly. Even while saying, "I should never." We all did, at about 11 p.m., and we were having a great time when there was a knock on the door.

I peered through the curtain, and O'Riley was on the porch. I let him in.

"Officer, come join us in a glass of bubbles."

"I'll come in, but I got news, no drink for me."

"Follow me into the dining room."

He nodded at Big John and Sylvia but spoke to me. "You remember the two men who helped you with the furniture from the shop on Royal."

"Of course, Giles and Ettiene decorated the whole place for me."

"Well, I got called in because the precinct got a call; Giles said they was out with some friends and saw who shot Simon. The station called me, but by the time I got over to Royal Street, they was both killed, close range, bullets straight to the heart."

We were all three suddenly sober.

"Do you have any idea how he knew or who it was?"

"No sir, but the ones upstairs are already saying this is the mob, but my gut tells me otherwise. I wanted you to know so's you could keep at your investigation."

For a short time, my body turned to stone. From the side, I could see Sylvia and Big John clearing the table, and I heard water running in the kitchen.

O'Reilly left.

I am not certain how long I sat there, but eventually, I felt a hand on my shoulder. It was Big John touching me, but Sylvia was speaking. "Mr. Evans, we put the food away and cleaned the kitchen. I am very sorry the party has to end this way but you be in touch, and I will pray for you on Sunday. It doesn't matter which God hears it; it only matters I will be speaking from my heart and asking for your protection. Will you be alright?"

"Thank you. I will be fine." I lied.

I walked them to the door, said goodnight and sat down on the couch in the front room. I heard Big John say, "I left my keys on the dining table. Be back in one second." He came right in; I had not locked the door.

"Come with me." I followed him back to the dining area. "My keys are in my pocket; I just want to say, everyone in this town got secrets; if looking in one direction don't bring nothing, look in the other."

When he left, I locked the door but did not sleep.

Chapter 17

In the morning, I needed to settle my mind; my only meditation was to hit the weights hard. Murder makes me angry; when people I know are murdered, I become livid. I worked hard and heavy 'til I was more sweat than body. I drank a lot of water and hit the sauna. Giles, one of the many attorneys who used the club, was there.

"I require your services, sir."

"Tell me." It made sense to set the murders aside for a few days until the town cooled off, until I cooled off. Running around with a head of steam is dangerous.

"I have a client who is considering divorce. "

I interrupted, "Sit down." I was tired of having conversations with some guy's bits dangling in my face. He sat down on the chair opposite, and I sat up.

"She came to me because she thinks her husband may be having an affair. He gets home late a few times a week. He claims he is working late, but she says something about him is always off when he gets home. It may be paranoia on her part. When she calls, he always answers the phone at the office. It's a small office, and his girl would not be there after 5:00; I need you to check him out and be discreet."

"What does he do?"

"He is an attorney as well."

"Give me a name and an address."

"Clifford La Pierre has a small office over in the Bywater, ground floor, so it should be easy enough to hide in the bushes and see through the windows. He wouldn't be the first man to entertain at his office in order to be available to his wife by phone. She would not be the first woman to imagine an affair either."

"I need the distraction; I will start Monday and bring my camera."

As I walked home from the club, I passed three jazz bands playing but did not hear the music. My brain was still too busy trying to process what had happened. I could have passed a gorilla in a tutu and would not have noticed.

On Monday, I was outside Clifford's office with my camera.

I found a tree with a good view. His secretary left promptly at 5. He made a phone call, put away a file, and left at 5:20. I followed him home to ensure nothing was up.

I waited an hour, and he stayed home—nothing to see here.

The pattern was repeated over the next two days. It was on Thursday that things got a little different. He made a call and closed the curtains. I came out from my hiding place, and there were cracks in the curtains so I could see. He undressed, but I did not see any indication a female was present. The next thing I knew, he was putting on panties, stockings, makeup, and a wig. He put on his heels and stared at himself in the mirror. He made an ugly dame, but this get-up was arousing him. He pulled out little Cliff and satisfied himself. I got pictures of all of it, thanks to the mirror.

Then he had to clean up and get his clothes back on. The whole process took a couple of hours. I followed him home, and he arrived at 7:15.

I dropped off the film Friday morning, again a tip for discretion. I was going to have to put in a darkroom. At 4, I got the photos and

I drove to Giles's office, LeBlanc and Sons; I assumed Giles was one of the sons. He was not old enough to be the senior. He saw me right away.

"I can say with certainty there is no other woman."

"So, was he working the whole time?"

"No, and I have the photos to prove it. He's a cross-dresser, it's a kink, and he gets off on wearing ladies' clothes. The only person he made love to was himself." I laid out the photos.

"Oh, my goodness. I cannot tell his wife this."

"As kinks go, this one is harmless."

"I suppose it is; let me call Mrs. La Pierre."

After the usual introductions, "...and Mrs. La Pierre, the detective following him, said there was no hint of an affair; he was indeed at his office and alone. A hint of feminine fragrance on a man can come from helping a lady with her coat or even sitting near a client who applies scent without discretion. You have nothing to worry about but are on the hook for $200.00 for the detective fees." Then, to me, "Take these photos with you and destroy them. I don't want them in the file and in the wrong hands. They can be used to blackmail."

I drove home. A transvestite distraction was what I needed; it got me thinking of this case in a whole new way.

I went back to the coffee house. I got a few hopeful glances, which were good for my ego, but I headed to the bartender. I got the coffee with whisky. A little Irish courage might help me prove my theory.

"You again?" He poured my drink.

"Me again, Ettiene and Giles. Do you have any clue who they were with or what they were doing before they went home and were shot?"

"Yeah, they were here with Reg; they had recovered a Gramophone from 1887 in pristine condition they wanted to sell him."

"Where would I find this Reg?"

"He went to Baton Rouge to stay with his mother. I think he was afraid."

"I can see why. Any chance you have a last name?"

"Bernard."

"Are any of the men here tonight work at the telephone company?"

"Yeah, see the slim guy over there with the group of 5? That is Martan LaPlante; he's with Ma Bell.

Martan was indeed slim, bordering on effete. He wore a black turtleneck and black trousers as if to emphasise his lean frame. I approached the table, " Martan, have you got a minute to chat?" His friends moved faster than roaches in the light, giving us privacy. Their assumption may have been wrong, but it saved me the trouble of asking them to move.

He held out his hand, not to shake but as if he expected me to kiss it. I ignored it. " I am John Evans, private detective. Forgive me for being blunt, but I need a favour I am willing to pay for." The idea of making a few bucks perked his ears up. "Can you get a record of every call made to and from the La Blanche house the night of the murder?"

"Junior or senior?"

"Both."

"What's the reward?"

"Five bucks, cash."

"If you are not a governmental agency, this is highly illegal."

"10 bucks."

"It will take me a couple of days."

"I have to make a run to Baton Rouge. I leave in the morning and will return a day or two later. Is that enough time?"

"Yes."

"Where can I find you?"

He wrote down his address. "Walk through the sideyard and come to the back door. I have half of a double, the left half. Don't knock too loudly, I'll hear. Sound travels."

"Thanks, good doing business with you."

The following day, I drove to Baton Rouge and checked into a hotel, unsure how long I might stay. I got out the phone book. Ten Bernard families were listed. I decided it was safer not to call; I didn't want to spook our boy, Reg.

At the third house, I hit paydirt. "Oh, do come in. Reg will be so happy to see a friend from home, and your timing is perfect. He is coming over for tea. What did you say your name was?"

"I didn't, it's John Evans."

"Mary Bernard, I am Reg's aunt. Do make yourself at home, John. He will be here any minute. You see, my sister just lives down the street. I have to run to the kitchen; I have cookies in the oven and need to get the kettle on to boil.

I sat down; nice place, plush furniture to sit on. Well-made cabinets, only the bowl of inedible hard candy on the coffee table indicated I was in the home of an older woman.

Reg came in, and his face paled at the sight of me.

"Let's step onto the porch so your aunt won't hear. We stepped out. "I can tell by the look on your face that you know who I am, so let's skip the introductions. You were with my friends Giles and Ettiene before they were killed, and I need to know exactly what happened. What you saw, what you heard, every detail."

"Friends," he mocked. "We are your friends when you need your house decorated, or a good haircut, or some new clothes, but fags are never truly anyone's friends. At best, we are tolerated. Tolerance is the most ugly word in the human language; it lacks all respect."

"That's not how I saw it. Yeah, I needed them. They decorated my place and did a great job, but I saw them as friends; we've gone out for drinks, and they were going to be coming over to my place for dinner." Eventually, they probably would have, so it wasn't a lie. He softened.

"Well, they had a gramophone they wanted to show me, and while it is not technically an antique, it was a pristine model from 1887. We were walking back to the shop; they lived in the back of the store. As we walked through the quarter, suddenly Giles shouted, 'Oh my god, I know who,' and he went silent as several women turned to look at us."

"These women, who were they? Do you know where they were headed?"

"They were in line for Mona's place."

"What's Mona's place?"

"It's a bar that has a weekly event for women, women who like women."

"You're doing great. How were these women dressed?"

"It was a mix of butch and femme. The butch wear men's clothes, and the femme wear dresses and makeup."

"Thanks, Reg, are you staying here for Christmas?"

"Yes, I always visit my mother and aunt for Christmas; they are both widowed."

We heard a knock on the door from the inside. Reg opened it.

"I heard you boys talking out here, and it is such a nice day. I thought, why not have cookies and tea on the porch today." She set the tray down and turned to me. "I do hope you'll stay."

"I am afraid I must go, but if you don't mind, I will try one of those cookies. The smell is driving me mad." I took a cookie; I took a bite. "These are delicious; what kind are they?"

"Snickerdoodles, an old family recipe."

"I thank you for your hospitality, and Reg, thank you for your help. I will see you, sir, after the holidays."

In my gut, I knew exactly what had happened, except how I could prove it. I stopped for lunch, and over a plate of fresh shrimp, the gears of my mind were working so loud I could hear them. We would see what the phone records showed.

Later the next night, I headed to the back door of my new buddy, cash in hand. He gave me an envelope, and I snuck off into the night. I closed the curtains, turned on my desk light, and did not see what I expected. There was no call from the coffee shop to the junior La Branche home. There was a call to the house, but the number was different from what I expected to see. This was going to be more complicated than I thought. I was stumped, and I don't like being stumped. I headed to bed but did not rest easy.

Chapter 18

The next morning, I went for therapy at the gym. It was the only way I knew to get rid of stress. Alex approached me when I hit the locker room; I had introduced myself a while back. The invisible people see the most in the business I found myself in. "Excuse me for saying to sir, but you look vexed. Take a long sauna and see if you can't uncrease those eyebrows. Here's an extra towel; sweat 'til you can't take it any more."

My buddies Martin and Ben were in the sauna. Shaking hands while naked had become routine. Men did business in men's clubs to exclude the women, the Jews, and the Blacks. This was the time and the world I had chosen; I would do my best to shake it up a little.

"Hey boys, what's the good word?"

Martin spoke first. "We have been listening to every conversation and have nothing."

Ben's eyebrows went up. "Do you think they know we are spies?"

The use of the word spy might have been hyperbolic, but I let it pass; these boys might prove useful someday.

"I doubt anyone has guessed. And your secret is safe with me."

"How is the case going?" They said almost in unison as if they had rehearsed it.

"I think I know who did this, but I have no proof."

They both had thoughtful looks for a minute and then Ben spoke. "Like in the movies, get all the suspects in the room and start talking; let them incriminate themselves."

"That is not the first time I have heard this suggestion. What do I do, just keep a police officer behind a curtain?"

"Exactly,"

I finally went downstairs and decided to try the athletic club's dining room. I ruminated over a plate of Shrimp Remoulade before heading to the phone booth.

I called my client and asked her where she would be on Christmas Eve. She was going to her son's house as I had hoped. I told her I would drop by that night. Her response was perplexing.

"Delicious." is what she said.

Why would it be delicious unless, and if that was the case, she must have known, and the rest of the gears clicked into place.

The La Branche family would never be the same.

I called Sergeant O'Riley and told him the plan. I asked him to bring three uniforms with cuffs with him. They would go to the side of the house and walk to the back. It was 75 degrees, unseasonably warm, and I hoped there would be enough windows open for them to hear the whole conversation.

I rang the front door, and Sylvia answered. "Merry Christmas, Mr. Evans."

"Merry Christmas, Sylvia. It's cruel of them to make you work on Christmas Eve. Stay close; you will want to hear this."

Sylvia walked me to the family tableau.

I was met with chilly silence, drinks in their hands. It took Brian a moment to go into auto-host mode and offer me a drink.

"No thanks, I won't be here long. For clarity's sake, I refer to the young Mrs. La Branche as Junior and the senior as Senior. Otherwise, we will never get this straight."

Junior stepped forward. "You do realise you are interrupting our Christmas Eve."

"I do, and I will be fast. I know you shot Potts, and I know you shot the boys over at the Antique shop for the crime of recognising you in men's clothes. They saw you outside of a weekly twisted sister event. I know you shot at me as well to warn me off, get me away from the gossip in the coffee house, and try to move me to your team, team crime of passion."

She stepped back and paled.

"I kept wondering why you were so keen on proving your husband and Potts were involved; I realise now it was so you could have a crime of passion defence if you ever got caught, but we both know it was not a crime of passion. But what I could not figure out was why."

I paused, scanning the faces. All three of them looked guilty as hell. "Why turned out to be money and Brian's reputation. You like this life, and you like this arrangement. But Brian did not call you; he called you, Senior. He was in a panic. Brian had confessed his desires to Potts and tried to get him to walk on the wild side, but Potts wasn't having it. He threatened to expose Brian to his mother." Senior paled.

"Of course, you knew mothers always do, but you didn't want a public scandal. You knew when you called Junior here you were setting her up. You didn't want the call traced, so you went to a neighbour's house and got Junior here, all worried she would lose all that money and status. You knew she had a gun, and you knew she knew how to use it. All grocery stores keep one under the counter, and a girl from the wrong side of the tracks would not hesitate to protect her interests."

Brian stepped forward, pretending to be courageous and gallant. "Are you saying that you are going to arrest both my mother and my wife?"

Senior spoke now. "Don't be ridiculous; he does not have a shred of proof. So what If I called, and so what if she murdered Potts and your little faggy friends. We are the La Branche family."

"So you admit it."

Junior stepped up to the plate this time. "I hired you because you were new in town, and I thought you would be a useful idiot, but then that bitch put you back on the trail; your job was to destroy me and give her the precious Brian back. Yes, I murdered all three, yes, she set me up, but the gun is in the river, and you can never prove a thing. Merry Christmas, and don't let the door hit you on the way out."

O'Riley stepped in. "Sounds like a confession to me, boys." All three were cuffed.

Brian looked like he was going to cry. "Why are you cuffing me? I didn't do anything."

"Aiding and abetting pretty boy, you may get out of jail before these two, but you will never be anything in this town again."

"I will still be rich, and that's all that matters."

Senior tried to wrest her way out of the cuffs, "I simply made a phone call; that is not a crime."

"Reasonable provocation; you knew what you were doing when you made that call." O'Reilly cuffed her.

I called out after Junior, "Cheer up, you might like prison. It's all women, which I have heard is to your taste."

My friends walked the perps out through the front door; I had given a tip-off to the paper so there would be a lovely photograph of the crime family on Christmas day.

Sylvia came up to me. "I have a feast all prepared; what do you say we sit down for some dinner before I go home to my family."

"Why not invite the family? I would love to meet the kid, and no one is here to scold you for sitting at the white man's table."

She hesitated before saying, "I will do exactly that."

She went and made the phone call, and when she came back, she said, "I guess once the new year hits, I will start looking for a new job."

"You have a job if you will take it. I have a phone being installed in a few days, and I will need someone to answer it. Perry Mason had Della Street to keep him in line. Come work for me, and I promise you will never be bored."

Tears filled her eyes. "I accept your offer," she said, holding her hand. I hugged her; it was that kind of moment.

Part 2 Chapter 1

January 2, 1946

Good whisky and wine with bubbles had played a big part in my life for the past two days. I was in a state of confusion when the doorbell rang. I pulled on a pair of trousers and went to the door barefoot.

Sylvia walked in. "Good morning, Mr. Evans. I am ready to begin my first day of work. I checked with the phone company, and they will install your line at 10 a.m. I expect you want to be dressed before their arrival."

I wanted to go back to bed, but I had Della Street on the job and had the distinct feeling my lack of discipline would soon be tempered. I was considering an escape to get some exercise when I was informed. "I have taken the liberty of making an appointment for you at 11:30. If you take this case, you will have to accept a lower fee, but I think it's time you did some good in this world." She wasn't wrong.

"You will be meeting with a Deacon from my church whose daughter has gone missing. If you head to the shower, I will take the liberty of making a pot of coffee, which I think you need."

"Yes, Ma'am." I saluted her and headed to the shower. I cracked the door before stepping out to ensure she was in front of the house. I don't think one should run around naked in front of a new secretary, but with all the mirrors in my home, caution was necessary.

Dressed, I followed the smell of the coffee and reached my office just as the phone installation man was arriving. "Good morning, sir. Show me where to put the extension in each room. I will wire on the outside and just drill through for the extension.

I settled on three extensions: two in the office, one for me, one for Sylvia, and one in the kitchen—none in the bedroom. I had no desire to take calls in the middle of the night. If it were an emergency, my bedroom was right behind the office, and I could get up and walk.

Sylvia supervised the phone installation, and I made a second pot of coffee. I wasn't exactly hungover, but I was not 100%. I thought about breakfast, but I did not want the food to battle the residue from last night's whisky, so I decided to wait.

Once the phones were installed, I got my number. **WH**itehall 7945.

I was feeling like a human when Deacon Bishop arrived. He blustered in and offered his hand, explaining that Mrs. Franklin, the choir director, had taken her car and would soon join. No sooner had we sat down when the bell rang again. Sylvia answered the door, and Vivienne entered. She entered her left leg first with a hint of a blue skirt, followed by a well-formed body that could only have been designed by a god. Lord, I may become a believer yet. The skirt was ankle length, and the dress could only be described as complete coverage that hid nothing. I felt like the world was moving in slow motion. My breathing had stopped. Her hair was styled like that of Veronica Lake, with a swirl on one side that skirted her eyebrow. She had that shade of coffee au lait skin that reflected light and appeared to be almost golden.

My rapture did not escape Sylvia's notice, and she squeezed my arm as she loudly repeated what the Deacon had said. "So,

Deacon, the last time you saw Elsbeth, she was headed for choir practice."

"That's right. She kissed me on the cheek, said good night, Daddy, and went off to practice."

"Is there any chance she could have left on her own?"

"No sir, Elsbeth was a good girl, a church-going girl. She would never take off. We celebrated her 18th birthday on Sunday after Church, and she went to choir practice Monday night as normal."

Sylvia spoke up. "Now, Deacon, you remember that trouble with a boy a few years ago? You need to tell Mr. Evans everything."

"That has nothing to do with today; she saw the error of her ways and repented fully."

I turned to Vivianne. "Tell me about choir practice. Was everything normal?"

"Completely normal. Elsbeth rehearsed her solo with the choir backing her up; just a few minutes before practice ended, she told me she had to leave. Female business."

I knew there was more to this story. I could see it in her eyes.

"I have forgotten my manners. May I get you some coffee, Deacon?"

I got up, and as expected, Vivienne followed. In the kitchen, I got a tray with cups and saucers. I heard a shout from Sylvia. "Cream is in your cooler, and a small bag of sugar is in the cupboard just above the coffee makers.

My Della Street was working out just fine.

Vivienne held one finger over her mouth to indicate silence and softly whispered in my ear. "I will return and tell you the rest of the story."

We served the coffee.

"This will not be easy; you will have to give me much more information besides an 18-year-old who sang well suddenly disappearing. I am going to need to talk to everyone who knows her. Let everyone in the choir know I will be at the church this afternoon and need to see them. Someone knows something.

"I will prepare a list for you and leave it with the church Secretary. Have you a pen?"

She wrote down the church address.

The Deacon coughed uncomfortably, "There is the question of your fee."

"There is an 18-year-old female potentially in a dangerous situation. I will take this case pro bono. When I find her, I will only send you a bill for expenses."

Much relieved, he got up and pumped my hand. He left in the same cloud of bluster he had entered with, and Mrs Vivienne Franklin left with the confidence of a woman who knew exactly the effect she was having on me.

I pumped Sylvia for information, but she knew little of the girl save they went to the same church; she was clean, well-spoken, and sang in the choir, and a few years back, there were rumours of trouble with a boy.

"I will head out and talk to some of those church members and see what I can find out. I will leave you here to cover the phones."

"Nobody has your number yet. You leave me with petty cash, and I will go to the printing press and have them make up new business cards with your phone number. Then I will get a desk and chair for myself and two chairs for clients to sit opposite your desk. If I return in time, I will assemble something for your dinner. I will not sit around waiting for the phone to ring."

"Yes, Ma'am." I got the cash out of my wallet, keeping enough for gas, along with a key for the front door, and left her at it.

I drove east to First Baptist and entered from the side where I assumed the office would be. I put my card on the table. " I am looking into the disappearance of Elsbeth Bishop for her Father. Mrs Franklin will let choir members and other folks know I am here so I can try to find clues as to her whereabouts."

She stood up and took my hand. "I am Loretta Mills. Widow Franklin has been phoning members, and many are already waiting in the choir room."

Widow Franklin? She was a young woman; I guessed that her husband was a wartime casualty.

"Loretta, if I need to speak to Mrs. Franklin again, where would I find her."

"She lives on the edge of town. If you are entering or exiting towards Nawlinz, just past the park is a small road. That leads to a housing development that never got fully built. She and her husband purchased the model home when the project went bust. I keep telling her to get a dog; it ain't right for a woman to be out there all by herself."

Loretta was my new best friend.

"Another question: do you have any ideas about what happened to Elsbeth?"

"I don't like to gossip, but I suspect a boy was involved. I used to be that age, and the excuse of lady problems means no one asks questions. I would use that excuse with my father, tell him I had to take to bed and then go out through the window. All young women know the value of that particular excuse."

"Any boy in particular?"

Two years ago, her father had a conniption when she went out with a white boy. He raised such a fit she never saw him again, but a wild woman is a wild woman. We just learn to hide it from our daddies."

She directed me to the choir room, where the coffee was brewing, and the members were chatting. When I entered, everyone got quiet, and one woman stood up.

"Hello, you must be Mr Evans. I am Bessie; I play the piano for the choir. The coffee will be ready in a hot minute; how do you take yours?"

"Black, please, and thank you."

I went around the room asking if anyone or anything unusual had been seen. I got nowhere; the parrots all repeated the same story; they never left the room; Elsbeth left a few minutes early, "lady problems", and no clues were obtained.

One by one, they all left, save Bessie and me. "I don't want to start gossiping, but I saw one thing in the parking lot when I stepped out for a smoke. Now, you keep that to yourself. Smoking and drinking are judged harshly in the congregation, and I have been known to do both."

"No one will hear it from me; what did you see?"

"A Buick Convertible Sedan in the parking lot, light cream colour. No one around here has a car like that. I went over to take a look. No one was in the passenger seat or even nearby. But that car is what you need to look for."

"Did you get a look at the plate?"

"I did not; I am sorry."

"Did you tell the police this?"

"Deacon won't tell the police; we know better than to call them out here. They are not friends with black folks. They will beat you as soon as they look at you."

Some things never change.

"Thanks; I think it's time I took a walk around and kept an eye out for that car."

I wrote down my number for Loretta in case she learned anything helpful and took a walk.

Little Woods was surrounded by marshland on one side and Lake Pontchartrain on the other. In the roaring 20s, it had been a jazz hub and a vacation spot. It was not a wealthy community, but I could see that everyone took some pride in their homes. Sidewalks were swept, and every house, from an old cottage to a more modern one, had bright curtains and flower pots out front.

I went from business to business, and no one knew a thing. Unless Elsbeth or her captor got in a boat and rowed away, she left by car.

The barbershop was the first bright spot in my day. They were surprised to see a white man but more than happy to give me a cut and neaten my look. I did not ask questions. Men gossip differently than women and asking ain't getting. I just listened. Lucky for me, the conversation was about that girl who disappeared.

"I saw that white boy's car from my window, the same boy she was hanging with a couple of years back."

"You think he came and kidnapped her?"

"Please, what you made of? When a girl likes a boy, she don't stop liking him cause her daddy disapproves. She just gets more clever. I expect she is holed up someplace uptown and will appear when he gets tired of her."

I couldn't stay silent. "Anyone know this boy's name?"

"No, sir."

"He was German, spoke German too; I heard him talking to his parents over at the Roosevelt where I work nights."

The Roosevelt was a grand hotel, and the location and the car indicated family money. Without a name, I would have to canvass the entire uptown garden district or ask Michael at the club. Uptown folks seemed to all know each other.

I arrived home just before six and hardly recognised the place. The office had been furnished with a second file cabinet, the chairs and desk as promised, and a beautiful Peace lily set to the side to take advantage of the light. I followed my nose to the kitchen. A pot pie with a note and receipts was sitting on the counter.

I had a little extra money and time. Chicken pot pie is waiting for your supper. I will see you at 9 in the morning. Be well, Sylvia.

Next to the note, 3 pennies lay on the counter. All cash accounted for.

The pie was still warm, so I cut a piece and sat down at the table. It was everything most pies wish they could be. The pastry was light and flaky, with just enough gravy to keep it moist but not wet. The vegetables had been finely chopped. I was looking forward to the leftovers while still eating my first portion. I remembered that this was the first food I had eaten all day, so I went back and ate the rest. Afterwards, I sat in my reading chair with the latest Ellery Queen and fell promptly asleep.

A knock at the back door awakened me. I checked my watch, and it was 9:00 p.m. I went into the kitchen and answered it.

Wearing a turtleneck and wide-legged trousers that tapered into her tiny waist, the Widow Franklin stood at my back door. She entered quickly.

"I hate to bother you at this hour, Mr. Evans, but I may be able to help. Bessie told me about the car in the lot, and I know who it belongs to."

"Come in and sit down," We entered the dining room. "Can I get you anything to drink?"

"Whisky, neat, Bourbon if you have it."

"I have it," I poured two glasses and sat opposite her.

"Tell me from the beginning, the very beginning. I need to know who this young lady is."

In between sips, the story came out. I learned that Mr. Bishop was a widower; his wife had died in childbirth. After her death, he and his daughter moved to New Orleans. He became heavily involved with the church for religious and community reasons and to have a network of females to influence and help guide his daughter. The Widow Franklin had been one of the babysitters and knew Elsbeth well.

"For her 16th birthday, I took her to the Opera. I wanted her to know music outside of Gospel and Jazz. She had a voice with those clear bell tones in the upper range and could belt at full voice in a couple of octaves. Music can be a black woman's way to move forward in this world."

"What opera?"

"Aida, it is not a happy story, but most operas end in tragedy. I love the music so very much, it didn't matter if she understood. I wanted her to feel it. At intermission, she saw this young man; he was as golden as she was brown, her eyes lit up, and his eyes landed on her; electricity moved through the room, and we all felt it."

I was feeling it now, but I kept it to myself.

"Acting as chaperone while two young people fumble through a first conversation is generally unpleasant, but there was no hesitation between these two. They communicated like two long-married people, even finishing each other's sentences. I am 14 years older than Elsbeth and...."

So she was 32, one year younger than me.

"I sensed he was older, so I asked his age. He was 22. I ended the night and told them that this could never be. Elsbeth was only 16, and black and white can't marry in Louisiana."

"You are mixed."

"So was my mother. My father was a white man, and my mother was not married to him. I am a love child. My parents live together on a small farm in the country. She pretends to be his housekeeper, but they don't fool anyone. I am Quadroon, more white than black, but to white folks, I am just a nigger."

"Not all white folks feel this way."

"According to Sylvia, you are an exception to every rule."

"What was the young man's name?"

"Dave Wagner, born in Germany and came to New Orleans when he was a little boy, maybe six years old. Smart, learned English in School, French too. His daddy had relatives in Lake Charles with a farm, who set him up in a butcher shop uptown, which expanded to having a bakery on the side after a few years. His Mama's breads are famous. I have driven to that bakery more than once to taste that Rye. She makes a sourdough rye that will make you weep with joy. With some good mayonnaise, ham and red onion, that will be a life-changing sandwich for you."

"Can I ask a personal question: how did you become a widow at such a young age?

"My Harold was military. I was married at 22 and widowed at 29. When the US declared war on Japan, he was called. He died on the aeroplane. Brain aneurysm burst and caused a massive stroke."

"What did you do?"

"I had grown up with music and dance; the church had just finished our building. They wanted a choir, and I wanted to work. It's a respectable job that pays enough to keep me in cotton. We paid cash for the house, and our lot is in an unincorporated area, so I pay no property tax."

She poured us both a little more whiskey. "My turn. You have no wife, no girlfriend that anyone has heard about, and from what I hear, you just dropped out of the sky one day, naked as the day you were born. You make friends with all the wrong people but still manage to do business with the country club set. Who are you, John Evans?"

I stood up, leaned across the table and kissed her. "Would you like to find out?"

"I am a good churchgoing widow, Mr. Evans..."

I kissed her again.

"Call me John."

"A woman like me can't just be heading to the bed of every man she meets."

I kissed her again.

"I am not every man. I am one man."

She stood up, I crossed the table, held her close, and kissed her again.

Somehow, we both lost our trousers and ended up in my bed.

Afterwards, lying close, I heard the most unexpected words.

"What am I going to do about my hair? If I sleep here, it will be a mess. Do you have a melon and a comb or brush?

Sylvia had been shopping, and I had spied a cantaloupe on the counter. I got it; she got up and placed the melon in a drawer on top of my things. She then removed her hair, put it on the melon, and combed it out.

We both started to laugh.

Her natural hair was very short, almost shaved and as vixenish as the hair was. I liked her natural. She seemed younger, more human.

"You thought that was my real hair."

"It is your real hair; you bought and paid for it."

We went back to bed and fell asleep afterwards. When I woke up at seven, she was already getting dressed.

"Why the rush? Your house is on a private lane?"

"I cannot afford a scandal. I will call you after 5 p.m. when Miss Sylvia has gone."

There were no questions, no when will I see you again, and no other nonsense. We both knew the answer to the question: as soon as possible.

She did not stay for coffee. I decided to hit the gym. I left a note on Sylvia's desk and took off.

Chapter 2

After working out hard, I showered and came home to find the smell of coffee and bacon wafting towards me, both incredibly enticing. Sylvia was in my kitchen.

"You know you are no longer a housekeeper and not responsible for my meals."

"I also know I will not be idle, and until that phone starts ringing, I am going to stay busy, and you are going to sit down and eat."

Within a moment of sitting at the dining room table, I had two eggs sunny side up, buttered toast and coffee; Sylvia sat opposite me with a cup of coffee. Her's was doctored with cream and sugar.

"We have a lead that may lead us to Elsbeth. I learned the name of the young man she was seeing, and I will head over there and talk to his parents. She may be uptown."

"If you find her, bring her to the church before you call the Deacon. Her Daddy will wring her neck if he finds out she ran off with a boy."

"Why don't you come with me? If the parents are at work, you can talk to Mom in the bakery, and I will talk to Dad in the butcher shop."

"No white woman is going to let a black woman question her."

"Buy some bread and see what you can pick up. I need bread anyway, and I hear she is a great baker."

Wagner Butcher Shop only had a smattering of customers, and I could walk right in. Sylvia had to get in line for the bakery; lines meant chatter, and chatter meant gossip.

I heard a man speaking German and assumed it was Mr. Wagner. I moved to the counter. "Mr Wagner?"

"Ya."

"May I please have a pound of those oxtails?"

As he began placing the pieces roughly the same size on the scale, I went on, "There are a few questions I would like to ask your son. Would he be at home today?"

For just a second, he froze. "David is no longer living at the family home, and I am unable to tell you where he went. We contacted the police, but things were missing from his room, so he went by choice. Is there anything else?"

"Two ribeyes, please."

The steaks were expensive but worth it. The fact that they had contacted the police meant that they really did not know where their kid was, but at least it was something.

Back at the car, Sylvia had some great-looking bread and an idea of what may have happened.

"Like you thought the women were talking about Mrs. Wagner's son. Rumour has it they ran off to get married, but I don't think there is a state in the union that would allow that. Also, Mr. David did not take his car. He took clothes and three suitcases, leaving the car behind."

"Does Elsbeth speak French?"

"She went to High school at McDonogh. This is New Orleans, so if she took a second language, it would have been French."

I had an idea. If they were in love, they would have to leave the US. There is no way they would have gone to Germany, and Wagner spoke French. How would one get to France in 1945? I began to think through my history lessons. If they were to try to fly, they would have had to take National airlines from Florida to New York and either board a ship or pick up an International flight, and those flights were expensive and uncommon.

I dropped off Sylvia and the meat and headed over to McDonogh. I made my way to the school office and saw the name tag '*Sarah Collins*' on the desk for the school secretary.

"Miss Collins, I hope you can help me. I am John Evans, and I am looking into the Elsbeth Bishop case. Are you aware that she is missing?"

She came over to the counter to face me.

"I have heard; it makes me so sad. She was one of our best students. She took extra classes over the summer to graduate months before her class. We had just issued her Diploma, and she had a bright future ahead of her."

"Do you have any idea of what happened?"

"Rumor has it that she ran off with a boy, and I have nothing to confirm or refute that assumption."

"Was she, by any chance, studying French?"

"Likely, but let me check her chart." She went to the files and pulled out a folder. "Goodness, A+ from first year on. Her teacher said she showed an uncanny aptitude for the language."

I headed back to the office and took a deep breath. When I got in the door, the scent was intoxicating. Sylvia was on the phone.

"Thank you so much." then to me," Oxtails are in the oven; they went in at noon, so they can't come out until seven tonight. Don't look, don't touch. It's enough for two meals, even for a man your size. You can grill steaks when you are ready for them. I got to thinking and made some calls, long distance, but I kept them short. Those two did not fly anywhere, and they did not board a greyhound either."

"Good work, that means they left by water. I will head down to the port and see what I can find out."

"Hand out some business cards along the way; I want this phone to start ringing. I will find something to keep myself occupied."

The port had one office with three desks, so I approached the only man who was not on the phone.

"If I were trying to trace a couple of folks that may have gotten on a ship, would you be the man I would talk to?"

"Yes, sir, every deckhand and passenger list lies with me."

"That accent is not New Orleans."

"Maine, I came down here after my brother died to help look after his kids, and you are a fellow Yankee."

"Chicago."

"Do you mind checking to see if a Dave Wagner boarded any vessel in the past few days?"

"No check needed. I remember him. He came in just before Christmas. He booked a room on a freighter headed to Marseille, a French company, not a proper cruise line, but they have passenger suites and a dining room, and it suited him just fine."

"Did he book just the one passage?"

"Are you talking about the black girl? She was waiting outside while he booked."

"Yes."

"Mr. John Wagner and secretary are how he booked it. This girl was no secretary and couldn't fool me, but it's not my job to play detective. The rich don't play by the same rules."

"How do you know he was rich?'

"Paid cash, didn't he? And there was plenty more where that came from."

He showed me the ship's records. Boarding was the evening after choir practice, and it took off at dawn. It would take just over two weeks to arrive.

"When is the next ship to Marseille leaving port?"

He went through pages and pages.

"Freighters only until March 11; that is your first departure with passenger accommodations."

"Thanks."

The wave of a hand caught my eye. Ensign Jacob was standing guard in front of Commander Martin's ship.

A swift walk got me to him quickly. "Good to see you. Is Commander Martin on board?"

"It's good to see you, too, sir. He is on board today, and I know he will be happy to see you. Come aboard."

Finding Potts' murderer put me in good company. I shook a lot of hands on my way to Martin's quarters. Our smiles were genuine as we greeted each other.

"Where are you headed on your next training run?"

"We are waiting for our orders, but a lot of what we do are runs to the Caribbean to keep the officers' club stocked with rum."

"Is anyone headed to Marseille or any port in France?"

"No. Why, what's up?"

I told him the whole story.

"If she is 21 and left without coercion, there is no reason to track her further."

"She is 18, which I have learned does not give her majority; she is still under the guardianship of her father unless she is married. I suspect she is married by now, but I need to speak to her Father before making any plans. I want to know what my options are, just in case."

"John, if you need to get to France, I will do anything in my power to make that happen. You may have to crew on a freighter, but I will help you find a way."

"Thanks for that," I handed over my new card. "I have a phone, so you can call me now. I also have a secretary who wants that phone to ring."

"Welcome to the modern world. Let me know what you need, and I will do my best to help make it happen."

Chapter 3

When I stepped into my house, the smell was incredible. The oxtails were cooking in the oven, and I smelled something else.

"Before you break your nose trying to figure it out, there is a fresh pear pie on the counter. You can pair it with some of that blue cheese I picked up and that port you hoard in the cupboard. I set the table for two."

"How did you...."

"Give me some credit, Mr Evans. A melon in a drawer—that's an emergency wig stand if I ever saw one. And if you have been dating long enough that her wig is having sleepovers, I decided it is time you should host her for a nice home-cooked meal."

"Thank you. We need to get Deacon Bishop on the line. I know where Elsbeth is."

Her eyebrows shot up, but she dialled the phone, got the Bishop on the line, and I took the phone. "Good news, sir, your daughter is safe; she was not taken. She made a plan to liaison with Mr. Dave Wagner, and they are in the passenger section of a cargo ship headed to Marseille."

His voice was so loud I held the phone away from my ear so Sylvia could hear him shout. "That is not good news, and it will not be good news until you bring her home. Running off to France with a white man, you get that girl home, and I will beat her with a switch until she finds repentance in her heart for such a sin."

"It may be a sin, but if she is married, all I can do is find her. I can't force her to return with me; I can talk to her and tell her how you feel."

"I lost my wife after she gave birth to that girl, and I will not lose my daughter, find her. If the expenses mount, I will sell the house. I would rather lose my house than my only daughter."

I sat with Sylvia silently for a few minutes, thinking how to proceed. I would have to visit the Wagners and tell them where their son was and with whom. Then, I would ask the commander to help find a way to Marseille.

"Big John will be here in a few minutes to pick me up. I had better get my coat...." *RING RING...*"Mr. Evans office.....she hung up."

"How do you know it was a she?"

"Not only was it a she, but it was a she I knew, and she did not want me to recognise her voice, so she hung up. Between the hang-up, the wig stand, and the look on your face yesterday, SHE would be the Widow Kennedy. You are not the only detective in this office."

"I won't cause a scandal, and I promise we will be discreet."

"You are a walking scandal, Mr. Evans, and a fast worker. How you managed to get this woman into bed the very day you met her is a subject I do not care to explore. Enjoy your dinner, and I will see you in the morning. Big John is just about to knock."

She opened the door, and there he stood.

"Hey, Big John."

"Hey, little John."

And off they went. Soon, the phone rang again; V was on her way.

V arrived with a scarf tied over her hair, which she removed in my kitchen. The wig was glamorous, but the natural look was more beautiful. We opened a bottle of Cabernet from Silver Oak Cellars, and I served the oxtails, along with some of the best bread I had tasted since I arrived into this year. With vegetables, the meal was complete. The carrots and potatoes melted in my mouth, along with the delicious oxtail.

"I was told to serve the pie with blue cheese and port. Can you handle a slice?"

She gave me a sly look, "Afterwards, we may need a snack."

Like Pavlov's dog, I had an immediate response and was straining against my trousers. Therefore, I had no choice but to remove them.

Afterwards, my brain began a series of mental gymnastics. To quiet it, I got up and sliced the pie. I lay the cheese on the slices and poured the port into the cute port glasses Nigel had picked out.

"That is the first time I have ever been served pie in bed by a man who is part Gorilla. Your back is the only spot on your body free from hair."

"No, the palms of my hand, the palms of my feet and my forehead above my eyebrows have no hair."

She laughed. "Don't forget, little Evans. He may live in a nest, but he has no hair on his head."

"When I am with you, little Evans gets all the attention he needs."

When the pie was finished: "I bought a toothbrush. I guess I will keep one in my purse."

"Keep it in the bathroom."

"I just don't want..."

"Sylvia knows. I forgot and left the melon in the drawer, and then when you hung up on her, she deduced it was a woman she knew, and that meant you. She is a good detective."

"The way you were looking at me, no detective was needed. The Bishop is generally obtuse and notices nothing."

"Tomorrow, I will try to find a way to Marseille. Bishop wants me to follow those kids, and that is where they are headed."

"Tomorrow, I have choir practice and will sleep in my own bed."

I slept contentedly. It may have only been a toothbrush, but it was a start.

We had a quick coffee the next morning, and I headed off to the gym. I put money on Sylvia's desk with a note telling her I would talk to the Wagners. I wanted to get them together before the opening of business. I figured 9:45 would get me there at the right time.

I worked out hard and ran into Falwell in the sauna.

"I have some work for you. One of my tellers at the bank just bought a house with cash, and I need you to find out the source of the money.

"What's her name?"

Penny Singleton is newly married, and the husband appears to have nothing but an appetite. If he has no means, the money came from her.

"Is any money missing?"

"There is an occasional disparity in the accounting for cash deposits. But I am holding my breath, hoping no one ever claims their safe deposit box was emptied. Jewellery can easily be converted to cash."

"Okay...I am headed to France, but I don't think it will be tomorrow, so I will nose around into Mrs. Singleton's affairs and see what I can find."

Once again, a naked handshake sealed the deal.

I arrived at the bakery just before opening and knocked loudly. Mrs. Wagner answered. I handed her my card. "I need to see you and your husband briefly."

"Ja, okay."

We stepped into the bakery. "Wolfgang," she shouted.

With no preamble, "I know where your son is; he is with Elsbeth Bishop, and they are in the passenger quarters of a cargo ship headed to Marseille. He has cash and plenty of it."

Mrs. Wagner turned bright red.

Wolfgang was oblivious to his wife's discomfort. "I thought they might be in a cheap hotel somewhere, and when he grew tired of her, he would be home."

"Where did he get the money?"

"His grandmother left him some in her will. He is 22 and can do what he likes with it. Sadly, we only had one son, but now we have none. A Wagner with a Schwarze Frau disgusts me. As a fetish, I can forgive it, but if he stays with her, he is nothing to me."

Whispering, "Mrs. Wagner, please step outside for a moment." a line was already forming for the bakery. Her helper would have to open alone. We went into a coffee shop across the street. I bought two cups of coffee and sat down opposite her... "Now tell me."

"My husband will come around; you cannot stop young love. Romeo and Juliet was a cautionary tale for parents warning us of this very thing. David told me his plan. I gave him the cash, and he signed a note allowing me to transfer his inheritance to a French bank once they are established in France."

"Do you approve?"

"My approval is not needed. My love and support as a Mother are needed. I respect his decision and don't care what colour my grandchildren will be." She began to cry, "Germany has shown the world what happens when you hate those who are not like you. I believe we have learned our lesson, and there will never be another war, but whatever happens, I will not begin a war with my son."

"You are one strong woman. You have my respect. Also, your bread is incredible."

She smiled at me. "Danke. I hope you continue to be a customer. You may come to see me anytime."

I did not return to the bakery with her, just in case the husband was watching.

I returned. Home or office, home and office, I should call it the house. I returned to my house.

"Welcome back, Mr. Evans. There have been no calls, but I have your note and will head out to do some shopping to keep you fed and spruce this place up a little bit before I finish for the day. I should tell you that Viv dropped by for coffee on her way home this morning. You are making her very happy. I will now be privy to all your business, but being a good detective, I am sure I would have learned it all anyway. I will get you some fish for tonight's supper; Viv has Choir practice, so you will be alone this evening. Save those steaks for tomorrow."

No words from me were spoken. Two women were deciding my life, and I was happy with the arrangement.

On the drive to Giles's office, I got some gas. I would never get used to these prices, .19 a gallon.

Giles saw me right away. "What can I do for you, sir?"

"Do you by any chance know Penny Singleton over at the bank?"

"I do. I handled her aunt's estate."

"Did Penny inherit?" Fallwell Duncan noticed a house purchase, and Whitney bank does not pay tellers an executive salary."

"It would be a breach of confidence if I were to tell you that her Aunt left a small fund in trust with this firm that gives Penny interest only, save the proviso that capital may be obtained only for the purchase of a house."

"I would never ask you to breach confidence. Unfortunately, I learned nothing from this office. I will see you at the club, sir."

As I was going to charge Falwell for the day, I wanted to pretend I had spent more than 5 minutes on his case, so I picked up Michael for lunch. "I am to have baked fish for dinner, so I need a real lunch; what do you suggest?"

"We will go to the Rib Room, where they make a po boy with prime rib. No one will look askance if you have a glass of wine to wash it all down."

And so we did. Michael was excited about his upcoming New York trip and told me all about his plans. He had written the box offices for advance tickets and had the tickets in hand for five shows. The train was not a fast journey, but he had a sleeper car arranged and would be bringing his married gentleman friend with him.

"There is a freedom in being a man, and there are no questions when two men want to share a room; they are always assumed to be companions or buddies. It is quite a different story with a woman to whom you are not married." He gave me a pointed look.

"How did you find out?"

"You have a neighbour who saw a grey sedan parked down the block two nights in a row. This morning, he saw a woman in a headscarf, a black woman, getting into that car. You are the only single man on the block, so...."

What was I needed for? This whole town was filled with detectives.

I told him about V.

"I could warn you that falling in love with a coloured woman will bring nothing but trouble, but I fear my words would fall on deaf ears."

"I will be leaving for France soon to chase down a case I am on so V and I can take a breath and see how we feel when I return."

"Your voice, your entire being, melted slightly when you said her name. I can see how you feel from across the table, and it's not likely to change."

I drove from lunch over to the port to see Commander Martin. He greeted me warmly.

"It turns out that I will need your help, Commander Martin."

"Patrick please."

"Patrick. Can you ask around and help me find a passage on A Freighter or anything that will get me to Marseille?"

"I thought you might be back. I made some calls. From this port no Cargo ships are heading that way until February. However, the Navy has a hospital boat that will soon be decommissioned and scrapped. They are selling off the fixtures to the French, and it is headed to Marseille next week. You may have to bunk with the crew, but if you can make your way to Florida, you can hitch a ride. The Port is Jacksonville, and the Commander is a decent fellow and an old friend. He knew Simon. I am sure he will invite you to dine with officers. The food is never great, but they have whiskey."

"Whisky helps. I will take a bottle along as a thank you."

"That's a Good idea; I have written everything you need here. It's a full day's drive, and the boat will leave at dawn on the 11th of the month. They are dismantling and removing part of the hospital equipment and stocking provisions until then. You are welcome to board anytime."

"I will have to move fast, thanks,"

I farted around a little bit, stopping in here and there, and hit the Whitney bank just before closing. I went to Fallwell's desk.

"The source of Penney's funds is a trust left by her aunt. She removed some capital and paid cash for the house."

"It's worth your service just to know for certain. Send me an invoice, and I will deposit the funds in your account."

"Thanks, Fallwell. It's good to see you as always.'

I returned to the house after Sylvia had left for the day; the space had been transformed yet again. She had a typewriter, paper, pens, and index cards. Flowers were on both of our desks.

I wanted company and realised Michael was the only real friend I had made, so I went to a local watering hole for a drink and exchanged bar conversation. The type that is meaningless to the point of inanity. There is comfort in the ritual. Returning home, I had my fish, vegetables, and rice. Unable to focus on a book, I took a walk before bed. It took me a while to find sleep. My bed felt empty.

While lifting weights the next morning, I realised that I would need Sylvia to take on a big project while I was away. I saw how much she accomplished in a day with little direction from me, and the phone and invoicing were not going to be enough to keep her occupied. She was too proud to accept paid leave just a week after beginning the job.

The Sauna held a familiar face, but thankfully, no one wanted to talk to me, so I lay down and closed my eyes. Sixteen days minimum to get to Paris. As much time as it took to find the girl and another 16 days back if I could find a passage or a costly flight. I would have many expenses, which went beyond the agreement to find Elsbeth. Theoretically, I had found her, and she was on a boat and probably quite happy.

I got to the house, and Sylvia was already there. The newspaper was on my desk; the news was all about the latest Nazi execution. I smelled coffee and bacon, so I went back to the kitchen.

"I have a big assignment for you today, Sylvia. I need you to head to the library and learn the dollar and franc exchange rates. Calculate my estimated expenses; assuming I arrive in Marseille, I may have to go elsewhere and add train fares, hotels, meals, etc. Call the airlines, and if I have to take a flight back, plan the potential itinerary. Prepare a report and an invoice to send to Bishop Deacon. Either he advances my expenses, or this folly of a trip is cancelled."

"Yes, sir, it will be my pleasure. I will take the streetcar uptown and get started."

I handed her the keys, "Take the car; it will be faster, and you may need to check some books out."

She was thrilled. I had come up with a few days' work, but I still needed a big project.

While she was out, I set up for dinner. I salted the steaks on both sides to allow osmosis to begin seasoning them. I then went out for candles, wine, and flowers for the dining table.

After I set that up, I went to Triple-A for the maps I needed for my drive.

Just before 5:00, Sylvia returned with a few books, brochures from a travel agent and an entire notepad. "Should I come in tomorrow and begin typing up this report? I am very used to working weekends."

"Absolutely not; you are fired if I see you before Monday.

Big John arrived a few minutes later, and she was off. While waiting for V, I began to look through the travel brochures. I suddenly had my project. I hoped it would be enough.

After a heavy dinner with wine, V and I lounged, relaxing and chatting. "I know Sunday is church for you, but how about Sunday night? We go out on a real date."

"You are crazy, ain't but one restaurant in all New Orleans that will allow a white man and a black woman to dine together, and Dooky Chase is closed on Sunday nights. Don't go courting misery."

I felt like I had been slapped. Misery had not been my intention. Romance had.

We were still in bed the next morning when I heard the bell ring. I shouted, "One minute," and grabbed a robe. I opened the door to see a tiny girl on my front steps.

"How can I help you, young lady?"

"You are a detective, right?'

"Yes."

"I need you to find my kitty. I fed him last night, and then he disappeared. Mom helped me check under the bed, in the closets and in the drawers, and we couldn't find him. Mommy says he ran away, but I hear him crying. I know he wants me to find him."

"Of course, I will help. Just let me get dressed."

I returned in a few moments, and my desk was covered in coins.

"Daddy said you charge fifty a day, and I have enough money for a day and a half."

I walked over to the desk, picked up the coins, and put them in an envelope. I took one penny. "Your Daddy was wrong; my kitten finding fee is one penny, no matter how long it takes."

She walked me to their house over on Rue Burgundy, and no sooner were we inside than her parents started apologising for her bothering me. I held up my hand to signal for them to stop. "Kitty finding is my speciality, and I am delighted to help."

The house was beautiful; the little girl had a street-facing room. "You never told me your name."

"I am Olivia, Mr. Evans."

"You can call me John, we're friends now."

I began the same checks, under, behind, and in, when I heard a faint cry. "Did you hear it, Mister, Mr. John?"

"I did; where did you hear it loudest?"

"Last night when I was taking my bath."

"Before we search the rest of the house, let's check the bathroom. What is the kitty's name?"

"Kitty."

In her bathroom, I called "Kitty."

'Meow'

"Kitty."

'Meow'

The sound was coming from the sink.

"Is kitty very small?"

"He's tiny."

The sink was pedestal-style, and I lay on the floor to check the plumbing situation in case I had to take something apart. The back of the pedestal was open for the pipes, and Kitty had wedged himself in the most awkward position, with one back foot caught behind the shut-off valve. I carefully extracted the foot, righted the kitty, and returned him to a very grateful Olivia.

She cried tears of joy. She took my hand and walked me out. I would leave it to her to tell the parents.

I expected V to be gone when I arrived, but I smelled breakfast. "Biscuits just went in the oven, so you have 15 minutes to wash up and shave. You have 5 o'clock stubble by noon.

I did as instructed and, with wet hair and a clean face, sat down to the most heavenly breakfast. It may have partly been the company but also the biscuits. Neither of us held back on the butter or the creamy, lightly scrambled eggs.

Besides the kitten's fate, we spoke little; enjoying the food and companionship was enough.

"I am surprised you stayed."

"I wanted to talk to you. I have been overwhelmed and overjoyed with the attention and romance. But," She held up a finger, "This can't go on. We can never get dinner in a restaurant, see a movie together, or have any life outside this house."

"But your father is white."

"My parents live on a remote farm, and officially, my mother is his housekeeper; she is on his payroll because that is the only legal way for her to live in his house, on his farm. I don't want to make those kinds of compromises, and I don't want to be a mistress to a white man."

"I don't think of you that way."

"I swear you dropped out of the sky from another planet because planet Earth, New Orleans, does not think like you. You will go to France as a single man, and have a romance there: forget about me. I am going to leave and take my toothbrush with me. I will go through the backdoor because we niggers don't be using the front door of a white man's house."

"You know I don't......"

"You are not the world. If I could love you, I would."

And she left. I cleared the table and went back to bed. I didn't want to be awake for what I was feeling.

Chapter 4

Monday came, but not soon enough. I needed to be immersed. I needed to be busy.

By the middle of the day, I had a check for the $500 estimated expenses from Deacon Bishop. Sylvia had spent the morning typing up an estimated cost invoice. I am unsure if I could have done as well without a computer. Armed with train schedules, exchange rates, the addresses of banks and money-changing bureaus, and flight schedules back to the US if needed, I packed a case and got in the car to head to Florida.

Sylvia had been tasked with creating a brochure and a list of services we would offer. Once written and printed, she would get it into the hands of businesses and others who might need our Agency. My casual relationship with money was ending, as she would create books for the company and account for every penny. I would be away for at least six weeks, and I dreaded the level of organisation I was to return to.

My drive to Florida was blissfully uneventful; I stopped for gas and meals. I saw the signs: No Coloreds, Whites only. I understood why V would not want to be the mistress of a white man. I still felt like crap. Rejection hurts, even for the right reasons.

I had slipped into this life so easily. I thought it was a sign from the universe that this was the life I was meant to have. I was beginning to realise that my good fortune had more to do with my gender and the colour of my skin than the universe.

When I arrived at the port, I parked my car, unsure when or how I would retrieve it. Maybe I should have taken the bus.

The USS Relief had red crosses painted on the side of the boat. I could not miss it. I gave my name to the sentry and asked to see the commander.

"We are expecting you, sir; come aboard." I was escorted to the commander's quarters.

"Commander Anderson. John Evans to see you, sir."

I went into his quarters. They were well designed for a tight space; I could see through the open door that these were also his sleeping quarters. It was like living in a small apartment.

"Mr. Evans, sit down."

"Call me John."

"Okay, John, Jacob here; welcome aboard. We have a minimal crew, just 100 men, a few cooks in the galley and myself. The French are buying the fixtures from the hospital and will use their crew to dismantle them. The other equipment is boxed and ready to be hauled off the ship."

"Thanks for letting me hitch a ride."

"It is not normal procedure to have a civilian on board, but your predicament was explained to me, and we are happy to help. We sail at dawn. The watchstanders get midnight rations; otherwise, breakfast is at 07:00, lunch at 12:30 and dinner at 19:00. Because of the small crew, we will all eat together, but you are welcome to join me in the officers' quarters after dinner."

"That reminds me, I have a bottle of Old Fitzgerald in my suitcase. I will bring it with me after dinner tomorrow."

"That will be welcome. The Navy gives us Wild Turkey, and it will be nice to have a change. We only have one Yeoman on board, Johnson, but you can let him know if you need anything. I will give you the grand tour and show you to your quarters."

The corridors were brightly lit and wide. The beds had been removed from the medical wards, and boxes were everywhere with equipment packed and labelled for sale. The operating rooms and laboratories were similarly dissolute. There was a sunroom and a library, both still in use. Considering how old this ship was, seeing its enormous size and scale was impressive.

"Now, here is the mess hall. The grub is pretty good. Every meal comes with milk, water or coffee." As young as some of these men appeared, they were clearly of milk-drinking age.

"There was a time when this boat would go through 7 tons of food daily, and the mess crew never got a break. This is almost a vacation for them." The comment, clearly intended to be overheard by the crew, got a forced laugh."

I still carried my suitcase, "So where will I bunk?"

"Because it is such a light load, I have a medical officer quarters set aside for you; it comes with a private head. Leave that suitcase here, and I will show you the crew quarters. Seeing those will make you feel like you are living in the lap of luxury."

He was not kidding. The crew had a crowded corridor narrower than the hospital halls, with bunks on both sides stacked three high. There was no privacy whatsoever. It was hot and airless, not a pleasant life. The toilets were long benches with eight holes on each bench; I guess you can get used to anything. The shower room was similarly crowded; there were two shower poles, each with four heads.

"There is a second head on the other side of the quarters, but even with a small crew, we must maintain a shower schedule."

When we got to my quarters, it did indeed feel luxurious after that glimpse at the life of the enlisted men. It was a little after 22:00 hours, and while I was not tired, morning came early on this boat, and I decided to get ready for bed.

I sleep on my back, and this bed was so tightly made I had to get up and loosen the stiff top sheet to allow room for my feet. I felt like a sausage being stuffed into a small envelope.

At 7 a.m., the alarm went off. While I had the feeling that freshly scrubbed, clean-shaven men would surround me, I just splashed some water on my face and combed my hair. I did not bathe or shave; it was too early for me.

When I got to the mess, men were lining up for food. The hot choice was pancakes. I have always hated flabby dough with syrup, so I went directly for the coffee. I was shocked; this was an excellent Brazilian brew. I expected, well, not this. I sat down at a long table.

I said 'fine' a lot.

"How are your quarters, sir?"

"How did you sleep, sir?"

"How is Naval life for you, sir?"

They were very well-meaning and earnest but damn young. Finally, the Yeoman came over. "Roger Johnson, sir, the commander is with control launching the vessel this morning, but he will join you for lunch. Anything you need, you see me, sir."

I laughed, "I just need more coffee." I was fully prepared to get up and get it myself, but my cup was whisked away and filled for me.

"Thank you, Mr. Johnson. Are there any exercise facilities on board?"

"Not really, but the hospital had a rehab room some men used, and you can always do pushups on deck."

Pushups on deck would suffice.

Showers, in one form or another, have existed since ancient Greece, but my room had a clawfoot tub with a handheld shower nozzle rigged into the plumbing. I decided to take a bath. The last time I had taken a bath was a lifetime ago.

The hot water was plentiful, and it felt good to be surrounded by the warmth. I could barely wrap my mind around what had been happening to me. I briefly considered that I was being housed in a mental institution, and this was all a fantasy, but then the water began to cool. If it were my fantasy, I would keep the water hot, so I stepped out into my current reality and towelled off. I had packed a couple of suits but did not feel the atmosphere called for a tie or jacket. I felt naked with only trousers and a shirt. How quickly I had become used to the uniform of my time.

I went to the library and grabbed a book. Gone With The Wind was the fattest book I could find, and I had the time. I had never read it. "Scarlett O'Hara was not beautiful, but men seldom realised it when caught by her charm as the Tarleton twins were."

It was the best opening line ever, and I was hooked. I read 'til lunchtime. When I got to the mess, I saw Jacob already sitting. He gave a wave, and once I had a tray, I sat opposite him.

There was a white chunky gravy poured over a piece of toast, green beans and applesauce cake. I sat down, looking at the mystery food.

Jacob laughed, "Shit on a shingle, made in your honour."

"What exactly is it?"

"This is the good version, dried beef in a cream gravy over toast. The cookie got creative with mushrooms, peas, and beef. Give it a taste."

While it did not compare to Sablefish stuffed with crawfish in brandy cream sauce, it was warm, somewhat tasty and comforting. The conversation was the same as in the morning. Everything was fine, and I appreciated the hospitality.

"This is an easy journey through the North Atlantic, not quite a straight shot, but assuming no rocky weather, we should arrive in 16 days."

"16 days of chipped beef?"

"The freezers are fully stocked, so this may be the last time you are served this traditional military delicacy, so eat up."

"Who wants my applesauce cake? "Hands shot up within hearing distance, but across the table, I had heard a meek 'Me, sir' coming from a slightly pale young man. I gave it to him; he needed the calories. The meek may not inherit the earth, but I could surely pass on my dessert.

Mr. Johnson appeared with coffee for me. I would have gotten it myself, but I was grateful.

"Sir, I wanted you to know we have a Rec room and a movie for each night of the journey. We traded with another boat, so we have fresh films. We have Going My Way with Bing Crosby tonight."

I knew of that film. Bing played a priest. We were a few decades before the general population began to equate priests with sex abuse. I had time travelled with my cynicism fully intact.

"Also, sir, we always have a doctor on board; see him immediately if you feel any symptoms, even a cold. Virus travels fast in this environment, and we try to isolate the sick."

"I will keep that in mind; thanks for letting me know."

The weather was not exactly warm as we headed East, but the sun was shining brightly. After lunch, I went to the deck to find a place to read. I got so immersed in the story I almost forgot dinner. Roast chicken, roast potatoes, roast Brussels sprouts—lemon pie for those who wanted it.

I headed to the officer's club. Jacob was the only person present.

"There must be other officers on board; a ship this size won't sail with only a Commander, will it?"

"The movies are very popular. As I told you, it's a small crew, but I am sure you will meet everyone as we go. It's our first night at sea."

We sat and talked over whiskey, and as I listened, it became apparent we saw the world entirely differently. I decided to keep my mouth shut; he was doing me a favour, and I had more than two weeks to go. I was beginning to realise it might be best if I kept to myself outside of mealtimes.

As the days passed, I read, slept, took long baths, did my pushups and passed the time. The military was much like I imagined prison to be. There was not a lot of privacy and little to do if you were not working.

Chapter 5

On Sunday, June 27th, in the afternoon, we finally pulled into the port of Marseille.

After my pro forma thanks and goodbyes round, I disembarked and felt free. I approached the first hotel I saw about a room for the night.

The desk clerk looked up. "Vous avez besoin d'une chambre, monsieur?"

Chamber, that must mean room.

"Oui."

He picked up a key and took me to a room for approval. The bath and toilet were down the hall, but the room had a sink. My needs were simple, and the room would do. I had to go out and change some money. I dropped a twenty and got over 800 Francs in return. I suddenly felt rich.

I paid in advance and went out to explore and see if I could find any evidence of Elsbeth and the man I now presumed to be her husband.

I stopped at a cafe and asked for a coffee; the tiny cup held about four sips. I knew to expect espresso, but this small portion made me sad. I had what was best described as a panic attack. Pretending I knew what I was doing in a place where I spoke the language was one thing, but what had begun as an adventure made me feel like a fraud. The girl was safe and presumably happy, out from under her father's thumb. I pulled out the photos of Mr. Wagner and Elsbeth and stared at them, hoping for inspiration.

When the waiter came for his coins, he saw the images and had a big reaction, smiling for the first time. "Ah les jeunes mariés"

What I heard was married. "Oui. Do you know where they are staying?"

He smiled, took the coins and gave me a blank look. "Je ne comprends pas l'anglais monsieur."

Thank god for cognates. I tried another tactic.

He was pointing to the photos. "Were they staying in Marseille? Or were they headed to Nice, Paris, somewhere else?"

"Oh oui, ils sont restés quelques jours ici, mais ils sont allés à Paris, elle est chanteuse et veut travailler dans un cabaret là-bas. Vous comprenez?"

Chanteuse, Paris, Cabaret.

"Merci, merci, merci."

I had a destination.

I tried to play tourist for a few hours. I love port cities; they are always excitingly international. As I walked, I heard snippets of many languages, and there was energy in the area despite so many businesses being closed on Sunday.

I went back to the cafe where I had the espresso earlier. No one was eating, but wine was being drunk, and while the cafe served food, I trusted the crowd. If the locals were not eating, I would find elsewhere to dine.

It is hard to believe, but there was a time when hotels took pride in their restaurants. I now live in that time. So I headed towards The Grand Hotel Beauvau.

As soon as I entered the dining room, I was aware of a pair of eyes on me, so I returned the gaze. Not a bad view.

Perfect grooming, her hair, makeup and clothes announced to the world she was not hurting for coin. The joint was busy. We just looked at each other while I waited for the Maitre de. He hurried towards me.

"I am sorry, sir, we are full; maybe you can wait in the lobby."

The voice, husky and deep, honed with whisky and regret, called out. "The gentleman is welcome to join me." English accent, London, one of the better neighbourhoods.

She knew I was no gentleman and was letting me know she was no lady. I took the seat.

"Thanks."

"American."

"Chicago."

"And here I was hoping for a mad Frenchman before I head off to Morocco."

"What's in Morocco?"

"Morrocans, presumably,"

I ordered, she ordered. We had the social conventions to get through. Besides, I was hungry. I ordered the bouillabaisse.

"It's loaded with garlic, and I suppose I should have it as well." Her intentions were clear, and I had just been at sea for 16 days with only men, so I was not going to refuse.

In a close-up, I could see she was in her 40s. I saw a wedding ring. I didn't care.

She talked a lot. She was married at 20 to a man 30 years her senior. But he had money. Just after WW1, she had a choice: marry cash or hold out for love. She made a wise choice. I didn't ask if she was widowed or just enthusiastic, but she was travelling alone and doing what she liked.

Finally, it came: the invitation for a nightcap.

We did what came naturally: I was using her, she was using me. It worked for both of us. Afterwards, I thought about leaving, but it was a nice hotel with a good bed, and I just drifted off.

I woke up in a cold sweat. I had soaked my half of the bed. Nightmare after nightmare, the past, the future, the self-doubt, all played out in the dreamscape. V appeared to remind me that we might have had something if she'd been born in a different place and time.

As quietly as possible, I took a shower and got dressed. I went back to my hotel. It was five in the morning. I lay down and slept for a few hours before heading to the train station. I had six of those tiny coffees on the way.

After making my way to the ticket window and asking for a ticket to Paris, I paid, and the receipt was tucked away. I found the train. It was going to be a six-hour journey. I wasn't hungry, so I just settled in my seat. I was still gripped with the panic that there would be none of the coincidences that had helped me in the past. I had no idea how to be a real detective. I didn't even speak French. I slept for a bit and woke up when I smelled coffee. An attendant was moving a cart down the line. The porter had a sparse collection of bread and pastry, a samovar filled with hot water and individual coffee pots preloaded with what smelled like freshly ground coffee.

"Voulez-vous une cafetière, de l'eau ou quelque chose à manger?"

I pointed to the small baguette with some ham and to the little pot with the plunger. Only a few francs later, I had real coffee. I pressed the plunger like the other passengers did and poured a cup. Espresso tastes excellent, but in the case of coffee, I prefer quantity over quality. Although I have to say the quality was not bad, not bad at all. The sandwich was a crisp baguette with butter and ham. I have always been a mustard guy, but this combo worked surprisingly well. I looked at my watch. It was not noon yet, but the journey was passing pleasantly enough.

When I finally reached Paris, I had no plan other than showing the pictures and hoping for the best.

The station had a reservations counter to help find a room. "Quel arrondissement préférez-vous, quelle est la durée de votre séjour et avez-vous besoin de toilettes privées?"

Grateful for the cognates, I spoke, "Toilet privy, oui. Arrondissement?

She pulled out a map of 20 areas. I pointed to number 18, high noon on the map.

She showed me on the map which metro to take; it seemed pretty straightforward on the 12 line.

When I got out of the Metro at Pigalle, I met a nice streetwalker who, with fingers and signs, directed me to Hotel du Clairmont. The street front had a bar, but down a little walkway, I found reception. I paid for a week upfront. The city had close to 3 million residents, and if I had found Elsbeth and Dave in less than a week by some miracle, I would drink good wine in nice cafes to fill my time. Rationing was still in effect, and while the city had food, menu choices were limited. I learned this at dinner, where my choices were Coq au vin and Potatoes Dauphinoise or eating elsewhere. I had to hand it to the French; the chow was excellent. They may not have much, but the artistry and care that went into preparing this old rooster was impressive.

I had shown the photos at the hotel and in the surrounding streets, and heads were regretfully shaken. Same with my waiter.

Disheartened, a second carafe of wine was called for. I would sleep well, or I hoped I would.

The next day, I walked and showed the photos to anyone who would look at them.

At a gallery, an artist named Jean Bouchon wrote down my question in French. "*Il est très urgent que je retrouve ces personnes disparues. Avez-vous vu quelqu'un ...quelqu'un qui leur ressemble"?*" Despite my rough pronunciation, I was understood, which got me nowhere.

Chapter 6

After a week, my back hurt from the hotel bed, my feet hurt from the continuous walking, I had a sore throat, and generally felt like two miles of bad road. I had nothing, not a clue, not a lead, not an idea. This young lady did not want to be found.

My room had a ceramic stove, fuel not included, after going out to buy some wood. I carried it back to my room, determined to spend one day in relative comfort. As the room warmed, I got hot water to mix with my bourbon from the lobby and sat and sipped, hoping rest and sleep would spark an idea.

Paris was rough after the war; women who might never have dreamed of prostitution were street walking just to buy food for their kids. With about half a million dead, primarily men, women were doing what they had to do to survive.

When evening came, I was filled with warm whisky and no ideas. I walked towards the top of the hill in Montmartre, cursing Mr. Bishop with every step. The kid may not have been 21, but married; she was the ward of her husband. I was on a fool's errand.

Feeling blue, I heard what sounded like a party. I followed the noise, and at the end of the block on Rue Tholoze, I found the party. I stepped inside a small, dodgy-looking bar at the block's end where the ghost of Christmas Present was holding court.

"Bonsoir." And the ghost became flesh as he stood tall among the crowd. Easily over six feet tall, he towered over the happy crowd in the bar.

"Boneswar." my accent was not good.

"Ah, an American. I speak English, my friend; welcome to PJ's place. I am Pierre Jean, and to whom do I have the pleasure of welcoming to Le Petit? "

"John Evans."

"Come sit with me, Mr. Evans; I rarely have a chance to use my English; what are you drinking?"

"Do you serve food by any chance?"

"Of course we do; I make my own charcuterie; when I can find a pig, all that remains is fromage de Tete, but with bread and some cheese from the goats at my mother's home, you will not leave hungry."

Settled with food and wine, I dined while PJ told me his story. As a young man, he joined the American Army and fought in WWI in order to gain citizenship. After the war ended, he worked at Delmonicos in NY, later joining the Cunard line as the Executive Chef for cross-Atlantic cruises. His English came in handy. He may have been the only French chef born in 1900 who spoke fluent English, so he took full advantage of it to build his career.

"How did you learn English, PJ?"

"My father came here as a Merchant Marine in 1889. He gave my mother the gift of my brother, so they married, and eleven years later, I came along. He was Cajun, French, and English, and from a baby, he spoke to me in both. Babies can learn languages without studying, and I hate to study. It interferes with my drinking."

We wore the night away, drinking and telling stories, until finally, "So why are you here, my friend John? Tourism is not so popular in Europe right now, and you look like a man with a mission."

He was easy to talk to, so I told him my story, at least the part that had brought me to Paris.

"Easy, place a classified ad in Le Figaro in English and French. Everyone looks at the classified ads, and someone will know them. It will save your shoes and remove that look of vexation from your forehead."

Cursed by my computerised mind, I did not think of this idea. "I will do it first thing in the morning."

I was not sure of my total alcohol consumption for the day, but at 4 a.m. I had to purposefully put one foot in front of the other in order to move and stop to steady myself without falling. Still, it was a productive night, and I may have made a friend.

Chapter 7

Pass out, sleep, what is the difference? At least I managed to undress. Surprisingly, I woke up at noon the next day with no headache. I headed for the shower and stayed under it until the hot water ran cool. As I dressed, I realised I needed to find a laundry; I packed up what I had in a borrowed pillowcase and headed out. I found a wash-and-fold on the way. I would have to wait a day to get it back, but it would all be clean.

The newspaper offices were easily found, and I had prewritten the ad in both languages (with PJ's help).

Urgently seeking Elsbeth Bishop. Please, anyone with information on her whereabouts, call me at the Hotel Clairmont. Ask for John Evans.

Recherche urgente d'Elizabeth Bishop. Si vous avez des informations sur l'endroit où elle se trouve, appelez-moi à l'hôtel Clairmont. Demandez John Evans.

I managed to place the ad just in time for tomorrow's edition. I paid the man, used my best French "Merci," and was on my way.

Already 5 p.m., coffee or wine? I chose both, afraid that the lack of caffeine would give me a headache. On the menu was a lentil ragu with sausage. A little bread and it made a good meal. The choice was always simple; food shortages were real, and what they had was what they had, menus be damned, but the meal was always excellent.

My gait was slow on the walk back as I contemplated what to do with the rest of my evening. Moulin Rouge appeared in the darkness. A few dancing girls might cure what ails me, so I bought a ticket and went in.

Champagne was included in the ticket, but I passed; those bubbles might give me a headache. A glass of water and another coffee suited me just fine.

Moulin Rouge had become a dreaded tourist trap by my time, but tonight it was earnest and lighthearted fun: a singer, the dancers and a comic who spoke French. I may not have understood, but the folks around me did, and I found myself smiling at their delight.

Jaded by porn, the topless Can Can did not arouse me, but damn, they worked hard. That was some excellent dancing. In bed by ten, the sleep of the dead was my destiny.

Grabbing a pair of trousers at the sound of the phone, I was downstairs barefoot and shirtless in a matter of seconds. The call was for someone else. When the clerk hung up, I used my best sign language. Pointing to the phone and then to me, "John Evans, I am expecting a call."

"Oui Monsieur."

I returned to my room and dressed appropriately; I drank a pot of French Press coffee and waited. No call came. I went to a bakery and grabbed a quiche, eating in my room, but no call; I went out, picked up my laundry, and returned to no messages. I bathed and put on clean clothes for a change, and there was still no call.

I wondered if they had left Paris or if my wording had been too aggressive, thinking and overthinking for three days, still carrying those damn pictures around, and no call came.

On day four, a letter arrived. A Paris postmark was addressed to me.

Mr. Evans,

I am a married woman, giving my father no right to return me to New Orleans. No sooner were we onboard the ship when the Captain wed us. I no longer use the name Eslbeth Bishop. I see no reason to call or to see you. I am happy to tell my father this was a fool's errand. Both my husband and I are working, and we have a nice little place to live. Please leave me in my happiness and do not disturb us further.

Formerly,

EB,

I finally had a clue: a postcode. 75006, the Latin Quarter, the home of the nightclubs where a young singer might find work. If her voice was as good as V had said it was, my bet she was working in one of the clubs in the quarter. I just wanted to talk to her before I returned, and I had mixed emotions about even doing that.

Heading out, I hit my first club. The hostess remembered seeing Elsbeth audition, and the dear girl spoke English. "Girl could sing; my god, she could sing. A voice was as clear as a bell. I wanted to add her to the program, but the club's owner is married to the girl singer, so there is no chance of that. She'll be on in a minute, white girl Peggy Lee wanna-be, which to me is just lazy singing."

"You sound American; how did you end up here?"

"My husband works as the assistant to the procurement manager of the American commissary here. Former military officer, his boss, Solan, insisted on the appointment. Life is good here. The commissary gets drop-shipments from the states so that we can get anything. Something you got a craving for? Come see me, Mr.?"

"Evans, and you are?"

"Dakota Johnson, I guess my parents wanted me to stand out from all the Dorothy Johnsons, so they went and got unique on me. I have grown into my name. My husband is also a Johnson, which saved changing it when we married."

"Lovely to meet you, Mrs. Johnson. Are there a lot of Americans here?

"A good number, military and ex-military mostly."

"It is nice to talk with someone who understands me. I have been using a lot of sign language. Any idea where this young lady is singing or what name she uses."

"Betty Rose, she even had a rose in her hair."

The name worked. I would buy a ticket to see someone named Betty Rose.

"Thank you so much, Mrs. Johnson."

"You are welcome, Mr. Evans; if you need anything, you come by and see me. We even have M&M's and Oreos."

"I will keep that in mind." If I had been wearing a hat, I would have tipped it. Instead, I gave her a salute and a wave. Mrs. Dakota Johnson had been very helpful.

Damn, there were a lot of music clubs in this town. Everyone recognised Betty Rose; she had made the rounds, and her auditions were memorable. Not finding anyone who knew where she lived or if she was working in a club, I finally headed home.

When I got off the Metro at Blanche station, a man was postering an abandoned building—a sketch of a beautiful young woman with a rose in her hair. **Betty Rose débute le Grand Écart 7 Rue Fromentin.** The date was only three days away. I was going to be the first in line for a ticket.

She was going to be performing right in my neighbourhood.

Whiskey, Wine, Water, other than coffee, everything I drink must begin with a W. I had three days to while away before speaking with the newly christened Betty Rose.

Dinner was next, and I ate what was on offer and was secretly delighted when my fish of the day came with white rice.

Since my dalliance in Marseille, there had been no women. I felt like I would be cheating on the woman who dumped me, the woman who did not want to be a white man's mistress. It was time to admit I had erred in my calculations. I thought I would live in a better time; the truth is we must all make the best of the time we are in. I chose a time of segregation in the States. I was going to have to cope.

The next evening, despite the fire in the furnace, I felt cold, inside and out.

I dressed in my coat and scarf and added a hat. I decided to go walking until I found something that suited my mood. I heard music near the top of the hill in Montmartre, so I peered in the window and saw a fireplace. I needed to sit by that fire.

I pointed to the fireplace and used my three French words and sign language. A lot of words followed my request, along with a perplexed expression. I walked towards the fire and saw the tables were full.

The waiter continued talking and gesturing. A mischievous man with a twinkle in his amber eyes smirking in amusement looked up at me.

"He is telling you you must share a table."

"I'll spring for some grub and a bottle of wine if you let me share yours."

With an exaggerated theatricality, he stood up and welcomed his old friend, which placated the waiter.

I pointed to the wine list, "Beaujolais Village if you have it."

"I am Pablo." There was no formality here, and I liked that.

" I'm John. Pablo is not a French name."

"I am Spanish, but there is nowhere on earth like Paris."

"You are not wrong about that; even now, as dirty and bereft as it sometimes seems, a charming cafe or bakery is around the corner, and the people are welcoming and very forgiving about my lack of language skills."

The wine came, and generous glasses were poured. We both took a moment to breathe in and savour the internal warmth.

"So John, do you have any language or only English?"

"Hayatımı öğretmenimi unutmaya çalışarak geçirmiş olsam da Türkçe konuşabiliyorum."

"Turkce, I have never visited. Are you from there or the US?"

A bolt of fear shot through my body, but a stranger in a bar would not be able to penetrate my cover story in New Orleans; I took a breath and a sip and went on. My father was Turkish, so I heard it in the cradle. By the time I said Mama, I was saying it in both languages. So why are you sitting alone tonight?"

The waiter came back, and tonight they had cassoulet, and since that was the only choice, I ordered it for both of us.

"Francoise and I have a very tumultuous relationship. She is with child and in many moods. Sometimes, it is best to remove myself from the situation. Do you have children?"

"I do not, not married, the lady I am most keen on; if we were allowed to get to that point, the law would intervene."

"If she consents, of course, you can marry; what law would stop this?" He was outraged on my behalf.

"Act of 1850 Prohibiting Miscegenation, which means that a person considered to be coloured cannot marry a person considered to be white."

Pablo looked at me carefully. "Forgive me, my friend, but you would be white adjacent at best. It is winter, and your tan does not fade."

"In the summer, I would probably get darker than she, but the people who make these laws don't care. All humans are the human race; that is how I see it. The rest are just shades of skin."

"How I see it, too."

The food came, and an iron cauldron was set carefully on a cork mat. A busboy brought bowls and silver, and the waiter served us, carefully removing the rabbit from the bone. We each had a nice portion of beans, sausage, and rabbit. The man in the kitchen was no amateur; this was the best meal I had eaten in ages. These were not Boston beans out of a can.

We ate and drank in blissful silence. Pablo was a nice guy, a little older than I, with more nose than face, but I had the feeling that head housed a lot of experience. That white hair told me he had to be in his 60s yet still had a baby on the way. I felt lucky to meet such a charming Iconoclast.

After the meal, the aroma of strong coffee greeted us, so I asked for some. Pablo declined. A drizzle began outside, casting a sheen on the cobblestones and making me more grateful to be seated by the fire.

Our conversation resumed, two men from different worlds; if only he knew my truth.

"Pablo, tell me, what do you dream of?"

"I dream of a future where there is no war, no bombs, and no more psychopaths running the world."

"I don't think that will happen, at least not in this century."

"You speak as a man who knows the world will never know peace as long as America keeps manipulating and profiting off of war."

"But weren't we the ones to end this war?"

He laughed, "Is that what they teach you in school? It is not true; Germany was lying in ruins when you finally came with your cameras to make propaganda films of American soldiers liberating the camps. Buchenwald was liberated by the US, but the British liberated the camps to the North and Soviets Auschwitz and many others. We owe our lives to the Soviets, not the Americans. Look at the support of Hitler by Prescott Bush and Joseph Kennedy as well as your car companies, Ford and General Motors. The Americans were Hitler's best ally until the public pressure became too much. Jews were turned away at your borders and refused entry. Only Palestine would take them in."

"I am certain that a plan will be put forth soon to help rebuild what has been destroyed and damaged." The Marshall Plan was at least a year away, but it was coming, and I was confident."

"All money from the US has a price, and they find a way to profit; nothing is truly given."

My instinct was to argue and defend, but he was not wrong. How naive I was to choose this time.

"I wish I had an argument, but I have none."

I heard a saxophone and knew the music portion of our evening was about to begin.

Pablo stood up. "Thank you for the dinner and the conversation, my friend; I must go home and, as you say, face the music." Stay and enjoy."

He shook my hand and went out into the weather.

I ordered a brandy, unwilling to leave the fire so early. The music began to fill the room, lulling me into a relaxed state. Three brandy later, I was very comfortable. I paid the bill and walked carefully in the wet night until I reached my abode. Sleep came easily.

Chapter 8

Finally, it was showtime. On the way, I picked up some Roses for Miss Rose as an excuse to go backstage. I arrived at the club early; I wanted to check out the setup and see how best to have a chat with Miss Betty Rose. The joint was tiny, with a bar on one side, a line of tables on the other and a little stage. It was more like a wide hallway than a club. I sat at the front and was prepared to share the table. As the crowd arrived, I realised this was like the coffee shop in New Orleans: all males. All checking each other out. Beyond ordering a glass of wine, I made no attempts at conversation. I just watched and listened. English was spoken by a few of the men, the ones with close-cropped haircuts, which told me they were military. Don't ask, don't tell was officially a long way off, but I would not tell. I have always felt whatever a man wants to do with his Cyclops is his business.

The stench of cigarettes was making it hard to breathe. I was the only man in the room not smoking. Soon, the lights dimmed, and one of the bartenders ran up to the microphone; behind him, the musicians set up. "Betty Rose chantera dans environ cinq minutes. Pendant le spectacle, ne fumez pas, ne faites pas d'asthme."

Ne fumez, Asthme, I understood well enough to know the smoking would stop during the performance. That was fine by me.

Once the musicians were in place, "Nous vous présentons maintenant Mlle Betty Rose."

A tiny woman in a blue satin dress with a white rose carefully pinned into her hair pulled tightly into a bun took command of the stage. Her poise and confidence were beyond her years. She opened the show with 'Wham (Re-Bop Boom Bam)', a Mildred Bailey tune from early in the decade. She sang the hell out of it. Tune after tune, carefully selected to show off her talent. More than an hour later, she closed with the Billie Holiday tune 'Lover Man Oh Where Can You Be', which resonated with this crowd. She knew who she was playing to.

Seeing no other way backstage, I walked across the stage with flowers in hand. There were two unmarked doors; one was likely an office, and the other was a dressing room. I picked one and got lucky. Mr Wagner answered.

"I am an admirer; may I meet Miss Rose?"

He was surprised. This was her debut, and fans were already coming backstage. Betty was seated in front of a mirror, removing the stage makeup.

She stood up. "Thank you, sir, what a kind gesture for my debut." She took the flowers. "Whom do I have the pleasure of meeting?"

I sat down to make it clear I would not be leaving. "Mr. Wagner, I suggest you join us."

He sat down and took Betty's hand.

"Mrs. Wagner, don't worry. I do not intend to take you back to your father or interfere with your lives in any way. Your dad is spending a considerable sum to send me here to ensure all is well. Give me something I can take back to the man. He has been stressed and worried."

Betty sighed, "A couple of years ago, my choir leader took me to an Opera; it was singing like I had never heard before.

That's where I met David. We wanted to court openly, but my father refused to let me see a white man, so we snuck around. I pretended to be very involved with the church and invented tasks that needed doing to buy time away from home. When it was the church, he never questioned me. If we had tried to marry in New Orleans, we would have been in jail, so we asked the ship's captain to marry us as soon as we reached international waters. We had a ceremony on deck, and the crew gave us a lovely party. I love Papa, but when Mama dicd, he tried to control my every move."

"He was so frightened of losing you he forced you away?"

"Exactly, I wanted a marriage, a family and a career, and I fell in love with a white man. The only way to be a wife and not a mistress was for us to leave. Tell Papa I am sorry, but I could not tell anyone, or they would have stopped us. I have meant to send a letter but don't know what to say."

"Think about it; I will carry it with me and deliver it personally."

I turned to Dave. "Your mother sends her love; she understands and supports you. Your father does not know the role she played. What message do you want me to give your parents?"

"I will think of something to say to my Father. How long will you stay in town?"

"No plans yet. I have notes on possible transportation written up by my assistant, but I have nothing booked. On another note entirely, Betty, you are outstanding. You commanded that stage like a veteran with poise and performance skills I would never have imagined from one so young."

"I had the best teacher. My choir director gave me so many extra rehearsals to learn new songs, how to walk and how to own the stage. I owe it all to Mrs. Franklin."

"Did she know your plans?"

"No. I wanted to tell her so many times. She was like a big sister to me, and leaving without saying goodbye felt so bad. She relies on the church for income, and getting her involved would have been wrong."

"Viv is a good woman, and she was perplexed by your disappearance. The whole community was."

"I should have left a note, but I was afraid Poppa would find it and stop me."

The quiet Mr. Wagner spoke. "Tell Mr. Bishop that I promise to take good care of Betty with my entire being. I have employment, and with the inheritance from my grandmother, we can buy an apartment."

"I can imagine prices are low right now; good for you."

We sat silently for a few moments. This wasn't an interrogation, but sometimes silence brings more information. Finally, "Mr. Evans, how did you find me?"

"I made the rounds of the clubs, learned about your impressive auditions, got your performance name and just when I was about to give up, I saw the poster for Miss Betty Rose. Part detective work, part dumb luck."

She laughed. "Tell my father, as soon as I have made my name, I do want to have a child, but he will have to wait at least a decade for his grandbaby. We are doing everything we can to hold off on that."

There was not yet a birth control pill, and I doubt Dave had gotten a vasectomy, so it was condoms or withdrawal. Both were dicey, but they worked for the lucky.

"And Mr. Evans, the ad in the paper scared me, but I am glad you found me. Make sure Poppa knows I am well and happy. Le Grand Écart may be the smallest music venue in Paris, but I know this crowd; they are the tastemakers; if they embrace you, the rest of Paris will follow."

A lesson Bette Midler was to learn decades later. "They embraced you. The applause was genuine, as was mine. How about I come back in 3 days, give you some time to write your letters, and I can figure out how I can get home. I will see the show again, and we can get a drink afterwards. Sounds good?"

"Yes sir, Mr Evans. I am going to change the show up a little bit every night. Is there something you would like to hear?"

"Anything you sing will be fine by me. If you played in New Orleans, I would be a regular."

"I hope to someday; that is my dream. Come back with a grandbaby for Poppa and a gig while I am there. If I get there, you will be a guest of honour. How will I find you?"

"Just ask around. Everyone knows my reputation."

"A good reputation is worth more than gold."

"No, I have a bad reputation. I worked hard for it." I gave her a wink, put on my hat and went out into the night.

I had eaten no dinner and hoped my friend PJ would be at his club. I wanted to let him know his suggestion had worked.

Walking in the door of la Petite, "Mr Evans, you are welcome, come and sit with me."

"Mr. Hayes, it's good to see you."

He introduced me to his friends. "This is Mr. Evans, a detective and an associate of mine from New Orleans. Make some room."

A chair was wedged into a crowded table. I joined the party. I ate, I drank, and I told PJ about the resolution. After that, it was just fun. We shared wine, and I had an omelette with a baguette. All was well in my world for those hours, and I was happy.

The following day, I sent a Telegram to Sylvia:

NEW ORLEANS LA 21 JAN 1946

SYLVIA WHITE NEW ORLEANS LA

TELL BISHOP ALL GOOD E MARRIED STOP BOTH WORKING STOP COMING HOME STOP EVANS

WORD COUNT: 11

COST: .66

When I returned to my hotel, the French Police were waiting for me." Please come with us, sir. The Préfet de police wishes to speak to you.

"Can you tell me what this is about?

I don't think they understood the question; I also felt I was not being given a choice, so I went off.

The station was thick with cigarette smoke. I had never seen an officer on the streets, and it was clear they all stayed at the station smoking themselves to death.

I was led to an office, and it was clear I should wait. A few minutes later," Bonjour Monsieur, I am Charles Luizet, and we had a complaint about you. "Are you in my city operating as a private detective?

"Who made the complaint?

"It is of no importance, and please answer the question.

"No.

"Did you place an ad in the classifieds asking Elsbeth Bishop to contact you?

"Yes.

"What was the purpose of this?

"I wanted to find her. Once she responded, I knew she was here, so I looked and found her. Any more questions?

"So you admit you operated in my city with no license or even the civility of an introduction to my office.

So that was it; I had wounded his pride by not following protocol. "I admit I was doing a favour for her father, a man who could never afford my rates, thus putting me here in a non-professional capacity. If I were here formally, I would first introduce myself to you and ask for your permission to operate in your city.

"I am soon to be leaving this job. There is a tumour in my brain. Is it so much to be asked to be treated with respect during my last days here?

Suddenly, I remembered the lessons from the future: this man was to die in just over a year. He will die from this tumour. My brain was moving around on the space-time continuum that forms reality as we perceive it. I almost lost it. I tried to keep my panic attack on the inside and stay cool on the outside. It wasn't working.

Someone brought me a glass of water, and I drank it. My vision and hearing clouded over, and I felt the pull of the tunnel that brought me here. I took a deep breath as if oxygen could save me.

Then it was over, and he apologised for causing such distress. I was escorted outside, and a cold wind hit me like a slap in the face, a slap I needed badly.

After booking a flight back on National Airlines, I had to find a way to get from Montreal to Florida and get my car. The ever-efficient Sylvia had furnished me with train schedules; I would have a night or two in NY and book a sleeper car to Florida. A 20-hour journey was not something I could get through sitting up. I was headed home, and it felt like home. More than Minneapolis/St. Paul ever had.

On the appointed night, I was once again at the club. Word had spread, and the place was packed an hour before the show began. I got a stool at the bar, the last one left. I had not had dinner, so I had only a glass of wine. I did not want to be too snockered for our meeting.

Betty Rose was even more magnificent. She had changed up her act and wowed the crowd, myself included.

Backstage, my two eager beavers were waiting. I began. "Which one of you dropped a dime on me to the local cops? Dave's face reddened, giving me the answer. "It was before we met you, and I feared you would try to take Betty away from me.

"Apology accepted." Each handed me an envelope. Both were sealed, which was too bad. I was eager to read the contents.

Betty Rose asked, "How will you get back home?

"I am flying into Montreal. I will spend a night, train to NY, spend another night or two, and then take a sleeper car to Florida, where I left my car.

"Florida, do you mind doing me a favour, in Florida, if it is on your way?

"What do you need?

"Do you mind coming home with us? I have something I want to show you."

So home we went. We took the metro; their apartment was in the 6th district. Once Dave and I were seated in the living room, Betty entered the bedroom and returned with a book. She handed it to me. Carefully pressed in the book was an envelope, a card, and a photograph. It showed a woman holding a young girl, and both were smiling and happy. I presumed the baby was Betty.

"This you?

"I believe so. We moved when I was five years old. This was forwarded to me a year and a half after we moved.

I opened the card. It read, *My dear Elsbeth, please do not forget me. I will find you someday.*

No signature. The envelope held a return address in Florida, Destin

"Do you remember her?

"Sort of, I remember being cared for when I was a baby and toddler.

"Did you ask your Father?

"Yes, he said it was my Mama's sister who came and cared for me when Mama died."

"Did you try writing the woman?

"We had recently moved to New Orleans. I was only five years old and not yet able to write. Two years later, in the first grade, I got a stamp and sent a letter, but it came back as 'return to sender'. Poppa said she knew where to find us, but I never got another card, and she never came for a visit. I can see in the picture that she cared for me, and if you don't mind, can you ask a few neighbours and see if she is still with us."

I copied the address. "May I borrow the photo? Without a name, I may need to find someone who recognises her. I promise to send it back to you.

"Of course, you may.

"I have to drive through the panhandle on my way home, so stopping in Destin is not a problem."

"Thank you so much, Mr. Evans." She stood up and hugged me. I shook Dave's hand and went out into the night. The night wasn't cold. The blasted humidity had lessened, making for a pleasant evening. On the way back, I may have stopped at a few cafes for a glass of wine.

Chapter 9

I slept well, and the next day, I went to the Villeneuve-Orly Airport. The ease of check-in and the lack of security were refreshing. I picked up a book; the flight was almost 15 hours long. I needed something to read.

The meal service was impressive: China, Silver, and good-tasting food. It did not compare to the plastic trays and garbage that would be served in the future.

I read for a while, slept for a while, and soon I smelled coffee. Breakfast was served—eggs, fruit, and bread, basic but well prepared.

I read a bit more, and then it was time for lunch. Surprisingly, it was a great sandwich, Roast beef. With the food shortages in Europe, this was surprising but delicious. Coffee, tea and water were served.

When we finally landed, it was early. The time change had done a number on me. I took a taxi to the city and found a hotel. Basic room and a toilet down the hall, but it has central heat for which I was grateful. This city was cold in the winter. I would be fine for one night. I took a short nap and then showered. Dressed in a warm coat and hat, I headed out to find some food. Lunch had been a short time ago, but I figured I would sleep better if I ate and got on the local time.

I did not go far; I was quickly cold, even dressed as I was. Again, there is a limited menu. Rationing was still in effect in Montreal. I was lucky to be in New Orleans, where there were few limits on what I could buy, and the local water yielded plenty of seafood.

Broiled Lake Whitefish seemed like a safe choice. It was served with a single carrot, a dinner roll and plenty of potatoes. Simple, good food and it hit the spot. Afterwards, I had a couple of brandies. There was no whisky in the house.

Sleep did not come easy, but I eventually drifted off.

I was up early to make my train to NY. It was a Fourteen-hour journey. I skipped breakfast, figuring I could grab a coffee in the dining car.

My brain kept going back to Betty's aunt. She cared for the child, so why was there only one letter? What happened to this woman, and why had Betty's father not attempted to reconnect with the woman who had given up her life to care for an infant after the death of her sister?

My book was quickly finished. The dining car featured some coffee that could have been better. I ate no breakfast but did try the creamed chicken for lunch. Tarragon and salt were the seasonings, which made it surprisingly good for a meal that looked like it had already been eaten.

We arrived in NY at 9:00 p.m. I got a room at the Hotel Pennsylvania near the station. Once I had checked in, showered and dressed, it was just past 10 p.m. The hotel clerk advised me to go to Joe Jr., a 24-hour 42nd and 8th Avenue diner.

I had breakfast for dinner, along with surprisingly good coffee. The bacon was quite welcome. A basic, good breakfast was what I needed.

Even with the coffee, the time changes caught up with me. I had a long, deep sleep.

I was in NY, so I spent a day playing tourist. I first picked up a ticket to Oklahoma for the night. After walking around all day, I treated myself to dinner at Delmonico's; I had no idea whether they relied on the Black Market or had an excellent supply chain. But they had a full menu. I dined on Oysters Rockefeller, a Delmonico's steak and creamed spinach. I had one glass of wine in order to be wide awake for Oklahoma.

I had never seen it, not even in revival. It was Impressive. I am not a huge musical fan, but it would give Michael and me something in common.

The next morning, I returned to the train station for my long journey. I booked first class. The train compartment was beautiful with polished mahogany, a table to pull down for coffee or in-room dining, and even a private toilet. There was no shower, but I would deal with hygiene once I arrived in Florida.

The journey passed pleasantly. Food was decent, but sleep was elusive. The train rumbling was not conducive to rest, and Betty's Auntie kept nagging at my brain.

Why would a woman give up years of her life to care for a child, send one card and then give up? I was afraid my search would lead to a cemetery.

When we arrived, I checked into the Seminole. After a shower, proper sleep, and a decent meal, I found my car. It started on the third try. The battery had some juice left.

The Journey would be about 5 hours, so I gassed up at the first station and made my way to Destin.

I got a map and went to where the address should have been, but there was no house. Just a bit of the burnt foundation remained. I feared my hunch about the cemetery had been correct.

There was little to this town. Village is a more apt description.

With no name and just a photo, I decided to try the neighbours. One woman was watching me from a window across the street. I started there

I knocked, and the neighbour responded quickly. "Good day, Ma'am. My name is John Evans, and I am looking for the woman who lived in the house across the street about fifteen years ago. Do you have any idea what happened?

"House burned down. That's what happened.

"What about the residents? Are they still in the area?

"They moved on to Pensacola; no reason to stay here. The one had a dead husband, and the other, she just showed up at her sister's one day. Why are you looking for them?"

I showed her the photo, "She cared for this girl when the girl was small, and the young lady wanted to find her, and I don't even know her name.."

"Hang on, somewhere I may still have the forwarding address. Jasmine sent me a postcard once they reached Pensacola at least twelve years ago. Set down, I'll be back."

Twenty minutes later, she returned. " I found it. No guarantee they are still there, but it gives you a place to start."

I looked at the name Jasmine Jenkins. "What was the sister's name?"

"Rose, friendly girl. They both stayed with me for a couple of nights after the fire. You can take the card, just tell them Mrs. Johnson says hey when you see them. I hope they are both well."

"Thanks, Mrs. Johnson. I appreciate the help."

Pensacola, open your....no Golden Gate I knew of, but whatever Pensacola has.

The drive was a little more than an hour. I checked into a motel before heading to the address on the postcard. I wasn't going to make the entire drive to New Orleans today.

I showered, put on a clean shirt, got a local map and drove to the address on the card. A beautiful, lean black woman opened the door. She was not the woman in the photo. " My name is John Evans. Are you, by any chance, Jasmine?"

"I am. How can I help you, sir?"

I showed her the photo. "This is the woman I am looking for.

She backed up and sat down. The look of shock on her face was unmistakable. "Rose," she shouted.

A woman of similar appearance came into the room, drying her hands on a kitchen towel. "Are you Rose?

"Yes, sir."

"This little girl is looking for you." She looked at the photo and crumpled on the couch, crying. "My baby, my baby."

"She knows you cared for her when her mother died, and she wanted to know her Auntie,"

Rose spoke first. "Come on in the kitchen, and you might as well stay for supper. We got some talking to do."

Over fried fish and salad, the story came out. Rose was not Elsbeth's aunt but her mother. "During the depression, I took in washing to keep my baby fed. It was hard work, but we didn't have much. Like everybody, we did what we had to do. I was married to Mr. Bishop and still am, to the best of my knowledge. Bishop was the janitor over at Istrouma. In 1932, they added a school and an auditorium. That man worked six days a week, and I worked all seven while caring for my baby. Times were hard, but we had enough."

"How did you end up leaving?

"I'm getting to it. Bishops auntie Ida Wells. She was a journalist back when women did not do that kind of work and wrote about the issues that mattered in our community. When Ida died, she left Bishop's daddy a little money. He put it in the market and made more, pulling out just before the crash. His daddy died in 1933 and left the money to Bishop.

"Why do you call him Bishop? What was his first name?"

"Ewart. Always used Bishop. He wouldn't let anyone call him by his Christian name.

"The money must have helped."

"Helped land me in the nuthouse. Elsbeth was growing and needed new shoes, so I asked for a little bit for our daughter. He refused, saying the bank was the only place for it. We argued, and I threatened to sue him for divorce and take my baby away. He had recently found religion and was talking about how he was the head of the household. As the master of the house, I was obligated to do his bidding. The next thing I knew, the men came for me, put me in a car and took me to the insane asylum.

Her sister chimed in, "Also known as the home for inconvenient wives.

Rose nodded. "Of course, I struggled and fought, which meant I was 'hysterical.' The first thing they did was shove a pill down my throat. They made zombies out of us, doping us up to keep quiet. Someone brought me a sandwich and a cup of tea. I had no appetite. I saw them going down the line, giving out more pills and making the women open their mouths and lift their tongues to prove it was swallowed. I have a gap in my gum where they had to pull a tooth in the back of my mouth. I shoved that second pill into the gap and lifted my tongue to cover it. They moved on, and when they was finished, I pulled the pill out. I held onto it til I got to the ashcan. I figured no one was going to sift through cigarette butts looking for pills.

"Did you escape?"

"No escaping that place, like a prison it was. Electric fence, dogs, guards with shotguns. I kept quiet and continued to hide the pills, playing along like I was all doped up. I asked one of the nurses if there was a chapel so I could pray." There was a chapel and a chaplain. I don't have religion, but I know how to pretend. As soon as she opened the door, I got down on my knees. As long as we were quiet, they paid no attention. She went for a smoke. I saw a door to the left of the altar. I got up and knocked, hoping for a chaplain. The sign on the door said the Chaplain came in every Monday for a service and counselling. I put my docile, dumb face back on and asked the nurse if she would bring me back on Monday. She told me she would bring me personally since I had been such a good girl. Here I was, a 28-year-old woman, being called a girl by a white woman.

"How long had you been locked up at this point?

"I do not know Mr. Evans. One day turned into another. My brain was on my daughter. I was just playing along. Monday came, and that patronising bitch came and took me to the chapel. Only five of us went. I faked my way through the service, and with my head down, I quietly asked for counselling. He took me into the office to the side of the chapel, and I dropped the act. I told him straight up what had happened and why I was locked up. He was shocked. The dope had everyone mumbling and drooling, and I spoke clearly. He promised to mention me to the psychiatrist in charge when he returned from vacation. Turns out I had three more days to wait.

"More coffee Mr Evans? Jasmine asked.

"Thanks," and to Rose, "How did you cope?

"I ate their sandwiches, drank their tea and bided my time. Finally, the psychiatrist called for me. I was calm and told him the whole story. He could see clearly that I was not crazy. He asked me to see him every day for the week. He needed a reason to release me for the records. It was that day I learned I had been there for three months. He would have seen me when I arrived, but he had taken a sabbatical and gone to Europe. It had been the nurse's choice to try to dope me up. The next day, I was not handed a pill. He had taken me off the medication list. I went for our appointments, ink blots, and tests designed to find even a little crazy. There was no crazy. I had never been more sane and determined. They decided to release me. When I got my clothes back, my wash money was still in my pocket, so I made my way home.

"What was that like for you?

"I went in the back door, ready to say I was home and taking my baby when another woman came at me asking if she could help me. It turns out that he left town the moment he got rid of me. The lady was nice, sat me down, and made tea, but she did not know where they had gone. I tried the post office, but they would not give me the forwarding address. So I went to my sister. I had enough money for the bus.

Jasmine interrupted. "And that's when I burned down the house.

"How did that happen?

"I was out back making soap. I would cook it over a fire in the backyard. I made soap and pies. That is how I got through the depression. People got to eat and be clean. Everything besides was a luxury. I had not seen my baby sister since she got married, and I heard her voice and went running to her. I was fixing to make coffee and sit down when the wind changed, and the back porch was all aflame.

"Did you call the fire department?" I asked.

"Destin Fire Department was all volunteers, all white, and when they heard a black woman's voice, they just hung up. Mrs. Johnson across the street took us in, and when the site cooled down, I went back in and got the fire safe and those cast iron skillets hanging there. Iron and steel don't melt in a fire: all family documents, photos, and cash was in the fire safe. We took what we had, made our way here and moved in to care for our great Uncle. When he passed, he left us the house. I still make soap but have gotten wise enough to put it on a fireproof patio. Rose sings at The Club Creole over on South Jefferson.

Jasmine continued, "Now you know my story, Mr. Evans. Where is my daughter?

"Your daughter goes by the name Betty Rose. She just got married and lives in Paris, singing at a club. She is one of the most talented singers I have ever heard.

Jasmine started to cry. "How on earth will I find the money to get to Paris?"

"I am afraid there's more. Your charming husband told Elsbeth you were dead, and the picture was of your sister who cared for her as a baby. She will be shocked to hear from you.

"Have you got a telephone number?

"I do indeed.

"What time is it in Paris?

"I think it is about 9 in the morning."

"I don't care what it costs; we need to call her, and I will find a way to get to her.

"I'll start the conversation and get her ready, and don't worry about the costs. Ask the operator for time and charges, and I will leave you the cash. Bishop is going to pay for this phone call.

I placed the call person to person and waited for the operator to call back. She would have to route it from operator to operator until reaching Paris. It took almost an hour, but finally, the phone rang.

"Elsbeth, this is John Evans. I found the woman in the picture, but she was not your auntie.

"Who was she then?

"Your mother, your father lied. She did not die in Childbirth. It's a lot to take in, but when you were a toddler, she asked for a divorce, and your father had her committed to a sanitorium. She was never able to find you. But she is here with me and wants to talk to you.

"My baby."

I turned to Jasmine. "What say we go in the kitchen and let them have their moment?"

A while later, Rose came into the kitchen. "The operator said that call was thirty-seven dollars."

I put forty on the table.

"Deep down, my baby must have remembered me. She is calling herself Betty Rose. I don't know how I will afford to go to Paris, but I have to get there.

"If you can get some time off, I have a plan.

I found a cheap motel and spent the night in Pensacola.

The next day, I took off with Rose by my side. The drive took about four hours. It was just after noon when I walked into the office. There were more plants and a stack of papers on my desk. Sylvia jumped up to greet me. "Mr. Evans, when you are ready, we have much to discuss. I have so much work lined up for you."

"First, let me introduce you to our guest. I hope she can stay with you for the night, but you must keep it quiet. This is Rose, Elsbeth's mother." Sylvia paled and sat down.

"Rose, meet Sylvia.

After the introductions, "Get Bishop on the phone. Tell him I have communication from his daughter and ask him to be here tomorrow at 9 a.m. Keep our special guest quiet.

She made the call. " Sylvia, It looks like you have been doing a lot of work, and we can go over that tomorrow. But right now, you would be doing me a great favour if you could take Rose to your house and lie low until the morning. Would you do that for me?

"Yes, Mr Evans.

"I will let Rose fill you in. Take my car; I won't need it tonight.

"Mr. Evans, I must tell you one thing before we get going. Viv got married, and the widow Franklin is now Mrs. Carver. Happened just last week.

This time, I turned pale and sat down. The whole time I had been gone, I harboured hope. The death of hope hurt as bad as the breakup.

Both women came forward and, almost in unison, said, "Are you alright, sir?

"I will be just fine," I lied. "It has been a long trip, and I need to rest. They left. I sat on the couch in the office for a bit and then decided to hit the weights, the only anti-depressant in my arsenal. I grabbed my things and made the walk to the club. North Rampart was not far, and I needed to leave the house.

I had not been working out with any regularity since I had left. Looking at a paper, I realised it was almost March. I lifted for four hours. Hard, heavy, punishing. Then I swam, as long as I could take it. I got an extra towel to cover my face and lay in the sauna. Just as I was drifting off, I heard voices.

Three voices. Giles, the lawyer I met on my first day here; Fallwell, my buddy from the bank—and one other. I could not pin the last voice. He sounded like a bullfrog.

Fallwell was speaking, "I heard he is back. He came back with a woman in his car.

"Probably a black woman. I hear he has a taste for dark meat," said the bullfrog.

Giles chimed in, "He has always conducted himself with the utmost discretion. Many of us have had dalliances, and he is not married.

Fallwell again, "Boys will be boys.

The bullfrog, "No white man should have a nigger in his bed. Goes against nature.

At this, I stood up. "You shut the fuck up, you dumbass racist. You are lucky, old man. I am going to cool down instead of punching your lights out."

Exit: Stage left: I went for the shower. Fallwell stood outside my marble shower enclosure. It was open on one side.

"Who was that asshole Fallwell?

"Didn't you get a look at his face?

"Barely, I was too angry.

"That was Judge Sprizzo, back from Europe.

After I got dressed, I stopped by Michael's office to say hello. I told him about seeing the musical Oklahoma and asked about his trip as I was leaving. "By the way, Judge Sprizzo and I are no longer speaking. Some disagreements are unable to be settled."

I was hoping that this would keep any questions at bay. I grabbed a catfish po boy on the way home. I ate, I drank, and eventually, I slept. I knew only one thing. For the rest of my life, V would be the one that got away.

Chapter 10

Shotgun houses have no doors between the rooms. The office bathroom was the only place I could be sure that Rose would be hidden while still being able to hear everything. When the bell rang, she closed the door. I answered it myself.

"Deacon Bishop, come in, have a seat. I have a lot to tell you.

"Thank you." he sat on the sofa by the side window.

"As you know, your daughter ran away and lives in Paris. The man you told her never to see again is her husband. She is singing at a small club and quickly becoming the toast of Paris. You may not like it, but that is her chosen life.

"Who will take care of me in my old age?"

"I can't answer that, but I have someone who will take care of you now. Rose"

At her appearance, flop sweat appeared on Bishop's face. He dabbed ineffectively with a soon-soaking handkerchief.

Rose spoke. "It has been a long time, old man. Unfortunately for you, the asylum did not think I was crazy. I did not have the money to keep looking for you, but soon I will have money and travel to Paris to see my baby first class."

"You are crazy; you have always been crazy. Where are you going to get the money to be travelling about?"

"Mr Evans has arranged an appointment for an attorney here in New Orleans. Fortunately for me, it is a community property state. Even more fortunately, you are a cheap bastard, so I know you invested that money you inherited, and I will get half."

Bishop got angry and started to shout. "This is proof of how crazy you are. That money is long gone. I ain't got a penny to my name."

I intervened, "I had an asset check run on you, and a friend is preparing an order that will be signed by the time you get home, freezing all assets until the divorce is final. You have what is in your pocket right now, so I suggest you sign those divorce papers the moment they are ready."

"You were supposed to be working for me. What right does that give you to nose around in my private affairs?"

"I did what you hired me for; then I did what your daughter asked me to do."

Sylvia stood up. "Deacon, I suggest you resign from your position as Deacon in the church. We need men of good moral character, not men who lock up their wives for being inconvenient."

I handed Bishop the letter from his daughter as he left in a bluster.

I turned to Rose, "What's the expression? Revenge is a dish best served cold. How do you feel now, Rose?"

"I am on top of the world thanks to you, Mr. Evans."

"Rose, before yesterday, had you ever visited New Orleans?"

"No sir, we stayed in Baton Rouge. I never got the chance."

"Sylvia, I can see you have been very busy, and we have a lot to discuss, but can we put it off for one more day?"

"Why, it seems you have successfully resolved this case."

"Everything I said about asset checks and frozen accounts. I was just bluffing. I need to call on some friends and get it done before that old coot decides to make a withdrawal."

Both women began to laugh.

Sylvia caught her breath, "You are such a good liar. That is both a skill and a handicap. Use your power wisely."

Rose stood up. "If no one objects, I will spend the day playing tourist until you find that lawyer I supposedly hired."

"Sylvia, take the day and show her around, please."

"I would be happy to. Come on, Miss Rose, let's go take a walk around the French Quarter."

My morning was spent at the bank, the courthouse, and Gile's office. He agreed to handle the divorce and quickly got the order to seize assets. It took a few hours, but my lies were made true.

I then dropped off the letter from Dave to the Wagners. Mrs Wagner hugged me and handed me a loaf of sourdough rye bread. She was happy for her son, and I hoped her husband would come around.

Chapter 11

Finally, I was filling the shoes I had pretended to fit when I entered this life. I had some expense money left from Bishop but did not offer to return it. It wasn't very much, and I had more than earned it.

Dressed and ready for Sylvia, I waited at my desk. 9 am, like clockwork, she appeared.

"Mr. Evans, you stay seated—my turn to talk. While you were gone, I set up a bookkeeping system. I opened a business bank account and had your buddy over at the bank transfer $500.00 into it. You were glopping all your funds together; that is no way to do business. The tax man does not like sloppy accounting."

"How did you....."

"White magic, I just said I was working on behalf of Mr. Evans. You are white, so no one questioned me. I also added my signature to the business account. Now, I won't be stealing money, but I had to pay for the brochures and the sign coming today to put out front."

She went on.

"I took the liberty of creating a price structure for you. Fifteen dollars for a basic background check, Twenty-Five for insurance fraud, and you still get fifty a day working for your rich buddies. Personal inquiries will have a deposit charged for expenses and a sliding fee depending on the means of the client. Do you agree?"

"Of course."

"Good, the fees are in the brochure. I will do the background checks; working for you, I can make the reference calls and local inquiries if they come from out of town. Don't worry about long-distance charges. They will be charged as expenses."

"You are amazing."

"You hired me to do a job. I expect that is what I should do."

The doorbell rang. It was the men with the shingle for the front of the house. They asked what I wanted painted on it. Sylvia answered. "John Evans, Private detective."

I corrected her. "Evans and White Detective Agency." Sylvia did not comment, but her eyes said it all.

I watched them paint my shingle through moist eyes. I had arrived. I was here. This was real. Thank you, Mr Kimball and Mrs Miles, wherever you are.

Epilogue:

Rose became a comfortable woman with over $50,000 in assets when the divorce was finalised.

In July she sent me a postcard from Paris. It said simply, 'Thank you' and was signed by Rose and Betty.

About the Author

Karl Wilder is the author of the comic novel Filthy Blond. He divides his time between Berlin and Paris. This is the first of the series.

About the Publisher

Vintage Pulp Press is dedicated to reviving the tradition of Pulp fiction